THE SPLENDID SABA SAGA ™

COMPLETE SERIES

VOLUME 1 - PARTS 1-6

DR. ARIEL SYLVESTER ED.D.

PRETTY NERD PUBLISHING

Disclaimer: This book is a work of fiction, and the views expressed herein are the sole responsibility of the author. Likewise, certain characters, places, and incidents are the product of the author's imagination, and any resemblance to actual persons, living or dead, or actual events, is entirely coincidental.

Hardcover ISBN: 978-1-958240-15-1
Paperback ISBN: 978-1-958240-27-4
Ebook ISBN: 978-1-958240-03-8

Library of Congress Control Number: 2022907246

First paperback edition September 2022

Edited by Winter Murray at the DePaul Writing Center
Book design by Dr. Ariel Sylvester, Ed.D.
Cover art retrieved from http://unsplash.com
Layout by Dr. Ariel Sylvester, Ed.D.

Pretty Nerd Publishing
2220 W. Maypole Ave
Chicago, IL 60612
http://prettynerdpublishing.com

Printed in the United States of America

Dedicated to my wonderful students. Always remember to Be Splendid. Special thanks to Winter Murray and the DePaul Writing Center for editing this book.

TABLE OF CONTENTS

PART 1: INTERNAL BATTLES

CHAPTER 1 - COMPLETION

"Sylvester, do you think our kids are happy?"

"Why wouldn't they be? What do they have to be unhappy about? Those kids are spoiled compared to the way we grew up."

"I'm not talking about things, Sylvester. I'm talking about reality. Their reality. Do you ever think they feel, I don't know, abnormal?"

"They are abnormal. We're abnormal. And your abnormality is intuition, so why are you asking me, Viv...?"

"I know I'm intuitive, but I'm still their mother. I still worry. What if they resent us for the way they are?"

"Maybe they will, maybe they won't. In the words of Morgan Freeman in *Lean on Me*, 'we don't have to do nothin' but stay black and die.'"

"Don't talk about death right now, and be serious. Please."

"Vivian, all we can do is trust God, guide them, and pray that He leads them the way He led us. We use what we have been blessed with to help others. We try to teach them the same. I don't know what else we can do. I'm sorry."

"You sound like Saffore."

"I know, I got it from him when I asked him the same thing the other day."

"Well why did you act like I was overreacting?"

"I'm just messing with you. But Saffore is a smart man. He's a pastor, psychologist, and a scientist. If anyone knows anything abnormal, he does."

My parents' concern is valid. They probably never knew I heard this conversation one night as I was ear hustling while they were in the kitchen. With my mother's intuition, I'm sure she knows I heard something. I know all mothers have intuition, but my mom's intuition isn't your mom's intuition. My mom's intuition is heightened. She's a human lie detector. A walking forensic with crazy discernment. So when she worries about my siblings and I, it's not a mother's worry, it's her anticipating something tragic she knows is going to happen. My parents believe our family "abnormalities" to be a "blessing," but sometimes I'm not so sure.

Who is my family, you may be asking? Let's start with where we reside. We live in Chicago. A place known for our amazing river, skyscrapers, pizza, hot dogs, popcorn, and architecture. We're also known for our segregation, high taxes, high crime, corruption, and gang and gun violence. My parents were born and raised here. My dad is from the

South Side of Chicago - Englewood to be exact. My mom is from the West Side of Chicago, in the North Lawndale area. They never knew each other until he started going to Morehouse and she went to Spelman, two historically Black liberal arts colleges in Atlanta, Georgia. Morehouse is an all-male college and Spelman is an all-female college. My parents met at a common spot in Atlanta through mutual friends. They bonded over being from Chicago, their mutual friends, and their "abnormalities." Their life long goal has always been to help those in our community, the Black community, by using their intellect from school, their wisdom and blessings from God, and their abnormalities from a friendly accident.

That friendly accident came from Dr. Saffore. He is me and my siblings' uncle, our pastor, therapist, family doctor, my mom and dad's best friend from college, and a scientist at the University of Illinois in Chicago. He is also an inventor. It was his experimentation one night in college that gave my parents their abnormalities. Uncle Saffore has this love for superheroes and comics. After studying comics and superheroes he felt that he could make some sort of elixir that would give humans temporary gifts. His plans weren't complete and as we know, young scientists aren't always the most careful. Back then, Saffore was known as the Steve Urkel of Morehouse. He and my dad were roommates. He placed the elixir in the fridge, and my dad thought it was some red fruit punch. Who makes an elixir red? My mom was visiting my dad that night while Saffore was away, and they drank the elixir by accident. After drinking, they were shocked at what they had experienced.

My father found that he could create force fields — expansive ones, around anything. He could use these force fields to make objects invisible. Or to protect people from being hurt. He's always been a bit of a protector, so I guess this power suited him. He uses this power to protect others. After college, my dad went on to become a lawyer. He uses his law practice to protect young Black boys and girls from being charged as adults for small (and sometimes big) crimes. We've come to find out that he can also mimic other abnormalities. So these abnormalities that my whole family has, my dad can copy them. They're not as strong when he does it, and he can only do them for a small amount of time. It's weird how he can possess his children's abnormal inheritances, but I guess we get our abnormalities from him anyway.

My dad is high yellow complexioned, 6'5 guy with a bald head, muscles like Jason Momoa, and a loud, booming voice. At times when he walks into a courtroom people think he's the person who committed the crime. Such is life as a Black man. But he doesn't allow it to stop him from protecting others. He wanted to become a lawyer because his closest cousin was serving 30 years for armed robbery. He died before his time was up. He was only 15 when he received his sentencing and committed suicide when he was

20. My dad felt he couldn't do anything about his cousin's tragic life, but he wants to help any Black kid he can.

My mom is a chocolate complexioned, 5'4 petite woman with long naturally, kinky coily hair, and a super toned body. With her heightened intuition, has the ability to sense when a situation will be harmful or when someone is lying, and she can pick up any skill without being taught. You can imagine how she felt as a college student when she could see problems before they occurred, when someone was lying, or knew how to complete a test or task in a matter of minutes. And it makes it hard for my siblings and I to keep secrets. I even remember before COVID19 came and tore the world up, my mom stated, "The world is about to turn upside down." I thought she was making a Hamilton reference from Lin-Manuel Miranda. But Mom was "prophesying," as Saffore would say. She couldn't explain how it was going to happen, or what to do, she just knew.

My parents realized that they could do nothing to erase their abilities. The powers that Saffore thought would be temporary turned out to be permanent. After many tests with Saffore, their abnormalities wouldn't go away. They decided to use their gifts to help their communities. They were focused not only on fighting crime in Chicago, but helping Black youth to choose other avenues to combat the disparities they face. After college, my mom became a teacher. She taught in Chicago for 10 years before she became a professor of Education at the University of Illinois in Chicago. She has now developed a writing curriculum that focuses on telling Black narratives. This curriculum is used throughout many schools in Chicago. She also works to make policy changes so that more funding and resources can be provided to predominantly Black schools in Chicago. She is my hero. Beautiful, courageous, smart, and awe inspiring. A TRUE QUEEN.

My mom and dad own community centers in both their old neighborhoods. They volunteer and mentor when they can. This is all during the day. At night they are the Michelle and Barack of super-humans. They have done and continue to do so much to help their communities. They are teaching me and my siblings to use our "blessings," as they call them, to help others in the Black community tackle the bondage that continues to plague it.

Who are we and what are our blessings you may ask? Well let's start with my favorite family member. Baby girl Allena, or Sassy Number Seven as we call her. I have wanted a little sister for as long as I could remember. She finally came, and besides being super cute she's also super speedy. She's faster than the speed of light and has an eidetic memory. This causes her to be a bit sassy, but she's the best seven year old ever. She is the same complexion as my dad with big brown eyes, a huge Afro puff on top of her head, and a tiny, but speedy little body.

Next are the twins, Calhoun and Wilson. Calhoun and Wilson are wild, rambunctious, caramel brown, 5'6 13-year-old boys. They are each crazy and annoying in their own right, but they have each other's backs no matter what. Calhoun has amazing physical prowess; he's a track star and musician. Honestly, he's the dopest one out of all of us. Dad calls him Ferocious Number Five. Wilson, or "Wil, son" as my dad calls him, is an amazing artist. He loves Uncle Saffore and wants to be a scientist and doctor just like him. We call him Sweet Number Six. The twins are the best dancers in the family and are popular on YouTube and TikTok under the name "Stanton Twins." I feel like they both got the best talents.

Even though we have abnormalities, it doesn't stop us from being human. Calhoun has sickle cell. It's a disorder that attacks your red blood cells, and it's mostly found in African Americans. Calhoun will have a sickle cell crisis and be in a world of pain. But he is the strongest person in our whole family. His gift of super-human strength is completely impressive. My brother can lift buildings, move buildings, and potentially tear the whole city down if he wanted too. We call him Samson at home. He loves this nickname so much that he has locs that he won't cut and he always has a snap-back on top of his crown. Different from Wilson who just has braids to the back at the top of his head.

It's like God knew that Calhoun would need someone to be close to, someone to understand him, and someone to help him. So my brother Wilson is a healer. When they were three and Calhoun was having his first sickle cell crisis, Wilson touched him, and then somehow Calhoun wasn't in pain anymore. Saffore told us that Wilson was able to hydrate Calhoun, give him warmth, and shift the shape of his red blood cells in the area where he felt the most pain. Calhoun still has crises, but Wilson can help him. Regular twins have this unexplainable relationship, but my brothers' relationship goes deeper than that. They can literally save and heal each other. Wilson is also omnilingual. I get so jealous of this because I've been learning Spanish since I was 4 years old and I'm still not fluent. Because of Wilson's healing and ability to communicate, he is always the star of our rescue missions. He's always able to heal and speak to everyone.

Then there is my older brother Bradley. Or Thrilling Number Three as my dad calls him. He's chocolate brown like my mom, 16, 6'2, a super-popular baseball player at our high school, and a robotics and coding nerd. All the girls want him. Yes, I'm a bit jealous of my big brothers' reputation, and I'm rolling my eyes as I write this. Bradley is invincible, I guess you could say. My mom and dad always knew that my brother couldn't get hurt. He would fall as a child and not get a scrape or a broken bone. It was like he was made of steel.

My mom and dad never wanted us to go on missions with them. They tried to protect us from that. But our grandmother, my dad's mom, urged them to allow us to use our blessings to help as well. Because Grandma said it, they had to do it. They decided to take us on a mission with them. Something small. My parents fight crime, but sometimes they just want to de-escalate situations, talk to people, and come to an understanding. My mom, dad, Bradley, and I were out one night and witnessed a carjacking. This happened when Bradley was 12 years old. It was a young woman being car-jacked and a 13-year-old Black boy carjacking her. The boy had a gun. My mom and I were trying to help console the young woman. My dad was trying to use his convincing ways to get the young boy to give him the gun. All I remember is that he called my dad a nigga and shot at him. My dad couldn't put his forcefield up in time. My mom was yelling, "NO!" and then the sound of eight bullets boomed through the air. When everything was calm, I saw Bradley standing in front of our dad, taking all eight shots. The boy dropped the gun in shock and fear, and my dad grabbed him. I'm sure Bradley jumped in front of dad because he thought the bullets would bounce off of him like so many other objects. Only this time, the bullets didn't seem to bounce off of Bradley — instead he seemed to absorb them. He said it was like they went into his bones.

My mom and dad took him to Uncle Saffore for x-rays. He hadn't x-rayed Bradley since we were babies. It turned out, my brother's skeleton was made of steel. The bullets were absorbed into his skeleton as if they were cells or bone marrow. My brother turned out to be a cyborg. My mom stood there in awe and said, "He's every Black mother's dream. He's bulletproof."

The boy that shot at my brother that night ended up needing to complete some community service hours at my mom's community center in North Lawndale. While he was getting help from my parents and completing his community service hours, he and Bradley became best friends. None of Bradley's other friends ever knew about his "gift", this boy promised to keep everything a secret. The boy's name is

Ahava. Well, it was Ahava. Last week at our high school, there was a school shooting. Who knew that a high school shooting would happen when high schoolers were finally able to go back to school after the pandemic. Eight students died that day, all of different races and religions. One Black student, Ahava. An Asian female, a Latino male student, a White male student, a Sikh male student, a Muslim female student, a Jewish male student, and the shooter himself. The person who did the shooting had previously put a message on Twitter stating his hatred for all races and religions. He also posted his belief in White supremacy and power, and his connection to hate groups across Illinois.

Hatred is one of those things that I will never understand. On the one hand you have Black Lives Matter and marching in solidarity with Asian Americans and Pacific Islanders. Then you have anti-everyone hate groups that storm the Capitol building. America is such a conundrum. It's like no matter how far we come, the hatred never goes away. It's like it's a demon or a spirit that no one can see. A monster that we must fight, but we don't know its weakness. Unity and solidarity just seem to make it angrier. And it hides behind humans who are too angry to see its presence.

My family and I were out of town visiting my grandmother in Florida when the school shooting happened. You can imagine how we felt that we hadn't done our part to protect the students at our school. A silence has swept over our high school. Vigils have been held in honor of those that passed. While we were at the vigil, all we heard was, "Where are our heroes?" and, "How could they not help us?" Most people think that being a superhero is cool and amazing and glamorous, but it's a tough job. When things go great, the world praises you, and when things go wrong, the world blames you. Our parents tell us to never tell anyone our secret of being superhuman unless we can really trust them. Ahava was the only friend that Bradley had that knew his secret.

No one in our family has felt more pain from this than my brother since Ahava was his best friend. This has troubled my brother's spirit. No matter how abnormal we are, we still feel human pain. My brother always wonders, "Why me? Why am I the one who can't be hurt?" I fear that my mom's intuition that we may not be happy is because of my brother's internal struggle. He wants to talk to me about it, but he knows that I already know what he's feeling. People call it empathy — people always try to define something they can't explain. But my gift goes beyond that. I'm aware of other people's feelings without them telling me. I can't read minds, but I can feel their emotions and see their memories just by touching their hands. Last week, after my brother's friend was shot, I held his hand and felt everything he felt. It's as if I had turned into him. I felt confusion, pain, sadness, and anger. I saw every moment he had with his friend as if I had been there. It was so deep that I stayed in my room for a couple of days, which is why I'm writing this. It helps to get my feelings out on paper when I'm focused on others. My parents thought I was just sad about what happened. I haven't told them about what Bradley felt. I believe that he should be the one to tell them. This has caused him to be withdrawn because he doesn't want to hurt me and it has caused me to be withdrawn because I don't want to say anything.

Last night, I had a dream, which doesn't happen often. It was Bradley sinking into a black hole, and in that hole were bullets and blood. I haven't told my parents or Bradley about my dream, either. If I did, they'd call me Joseph from the Bible and say I was seeing something that was really going to happen. But am I? I don't want to trouble my parents or bring extra unwanted attention to Bradley. I know that eventually, I will tell them. It's hard for me to be dishonest when I know what someone is feeling. My mom will eventually see that I'm keeping something from her anyway. I don't want to betray my brother's trust but I don't want to lie to my parents, either. Being a 15-year-old Black girl with "abnormalities" is hard enough. Not to mention being a nerd. A writer who spends more time in books than on Instagram. Fierce Number Four and not the life of the party at all.

My family is Black, prideful, abnormal, loving, and dysfunctional. We're trying to help the city of Chicago, and we seek help from Uncle Saffore on this journey. He gives us as much knowledge as he can. We have each other's backs, but our gifts are becoming a struggle. I'm only 15 — I don't want to do this for the rest of my life. Am I cut out for this? Do I just feel this way because of Bradley and the school shooting? I don't know what to feel. My dad says 7 represents completion, perfection, exoneration, healing, and fulfillment of promises and oaths in the Bible. He feels that our family represents all these things because there are seven of us. He calls us "Splendid Saba." Saba is Swahili for seven, as Wilson would say. Sometimes though, I feel like our life isn't so splendid.

"Alicia! Dinner is ready, girl. Come eat. Get out of that room."

My mom is calling. Tensions are high tonight at the Stanton household. Let's see how dinner will be.

CHAPTER 2 · HEALING

"Chicago has never seen anything like this. Hundreds of students hold vigils in honor of the eight students that died during the school shooting at John Lewis High School. This school shooting, or hate crime, comes as a shock to all, especially after many high schools voted to change their names to prominent heroes from all racial and ethnic communities, stripping them of their previous names of historical figures who owned Black slaves and committed genocide of Native people. The mayor had this to say about the school shooting..."

"Wilson, can you please turn that off? It's time to eat dinner anyway. And I think our family has heard enough about it," my mom said as my younger siblings' faces were glued to the television in our living room. The local news had been broadcasting this story every day for the past week. It was sickening and hurtful, but the sad part was, we weren't there to save anyone. With Chicago having so much gang and gun violence, along with the pandemic, you would think the last thing anyone would want to do is kill other kids. We were at our dinner table in our dining room. Between eating the soul food dinner that my mom tried to make to cheer everyone up, you could hear forks hitting plates, deep sighs because of the sadness we all felt, and when someone finally did eat their food, you heard the sound of food swishing around in their mouth. It wasn't a normal day at our family dinner table. We were usually laughing, talking, discussing our powers and what happened that day. I guess the silence started to get to my younger siblings and then the questions started.

"Mommy, Daddy, why do people hate people?" For Allena to be so smart, you would think she already knew the answer to this. And with my parents being Black, you would think they did too.

"Well baby, uh…" my mom started out, dropping her fork.

"It's because…" my dad began to finish looking across the table at my mother.

"People hate, Allena, because of differences. We as humans are always looking at our differences whether that be color, money, beliefs, height, anything. We're constantly focusing on ways that we are different. Instead of celebrating those differences, we hate each other for them. It has to do with our own insecurities," Bradley said this as he stared down at his plate, hunched over it, and slid the noodles of his macaroni and cheese around. He didn't look at Allena when he said this, and said it in such a monotone voice. His hood was over his face, which usually never happens at the dinner table, but because of the circumstances my parents allowed it.

"Is that true, Daddy?" Allena asked.

"Well baby, yeah. I'm sure there is more to it than that, but that's a big piece of it," my dad responded.

"Well what's the more?" Allena and her questions always stumped my parents.

"It's, well…" My dad continued before he was interrupted by my little brothers.

"Well I think people hate what they can't understand or control. Or if it's something that they fear," Calhoun started out. "Like I don't understand biology sometimes, so I hate it. I can't seem to take control of it, and I fear taking a test on it. So I hate it."

"Bro, you crazy? Biology is easy. It's gym that I hate," Wilson began to say. "I also think people hate because they don't love. You can't hate something that you love."

"Whatever the reason, Allena, we should've been there to protect everyone. Had we been there, everyone would still be here," Bradley said as he got up from the table. "I'm not hungry, I'm going to go for a run.".

"Baby, we should've been there but you can't keep beating yourself up about not being there," my mom grabbed Bradley's hand. Bradley had his hoodie on. He always wore his hoodie to hide his face when he was sad. My parents didn't see the tears welling up in his eyes, but I did.

"I know, Ma. I'll be back in an hour," Bradley said with his head down so my mother couldn't see his tears.

"You want me to come with you, Son?" my dad asked. I could tell by his voice that he wanted Bradley to say yes.

"Naw Dad, I just wanna run by myself today," Bradley hid behind his hoodie and began to exit the dining room.

"Okay, Son. Aye, take the hoodie off while you run, and don't run too far," my dad said. My dad always seemed to worry about Bradley when he went outside alone.

"Alicia, what do you think? You didn't say anything," Allena asked me. Of course being my little shadow, she wanted to hear from me.

"I don't know, Lena, I think hatred is a monster that plagues our world. And racial hatred is a little more complicated because we can't seem to get away from it," I didn't look at her when I said this. I kept my head down and dipped my fork in my macaroni and cheese like my brother.

"You think it's a monster? Monsters aren't real, Ali." I guess she didn't like my answer too much. Not as profound, I guess.

"Alicia, you have been a bit quiet since this whole thing happened. How are you feeling?" My mom asked me in that intuitive voice. Because I was holding on to everyone else's emotions, I hated for people to ask me how I'm feeling. Sometimes I'm confused whether the feelings are my own - or am I just feeling what someone else felt. Do I feel guilty because Bradley felt guilty? Am I sad because so many other people felt sadness? I mean, I'm supposed to be sad, right?

"I don't know what or how to feel. I guess I feel guilty knowing that we could've helped but weren't there too. I feel a bit confused about everything. Upset that it was our school, our friends, and that we're still going through this today. I mean, I thought most of this would end with our generation."

"Well I think before you kids go back to school next week, we should probably see Saffore and schedule a family therapy session with him. Maybe that'll help." My dad always felt that Uncle Saffore would have all the answers. I mean, he is a smart man.

The next week we all went to see Uncle Saffore at his lab in a suburb in Illinois. Bradley and I had missed school for a week and a half since the shooting happened. Calhoun, Wilson, and Allena went to school every day, but they were still a bit confused about everything. There has been a big rain cloud over the Stanton home since our school shooting. We all felt guilty about not protecting everyone, especially Ahava.

“Welcome, nieces and nephews, my brother and sister. I guess we’ll have this session today and y’all can tell me why we’re here,” Uncle Saffore said. No matter how sad anyone else was, Saffore was always happy and cheerful. I just don’t understand how this man could be happy all the time. This 6’0 dark chocolate man in reading glasses stayed in a button down shirt, a sweater over it, jeans, and J’s. He had waves in his hair, no beard, and you would think that he was 25, but he was 45 like my parents. With his pearly white smile, he sat waiting for us to respond.

“We’re here today, Saffore, because since the school shooting, we’ve been struggling to cope as a family. We feel guilty for not being present and helping. We’ve lost people that we love, and with the race piece, we’re having a hard time processing everything. A lot of questions have happened at the dinner table over the past few days. We all just need some clarity," my mom chimed in. There was that intuitive gift. She basically summed up the entire family's feelings in a couple of sentences.

"Take that hoodie off, boy," my dad whispered to Bradley, who just sat there with his arms folded. He sighed, but took the hoodie off and leaned forward.

"Well, what you all need to understand is that you're not going to win every battle. Part of having gifts and using them for good means that there are some battles you're not going to be present for. I understand your feelings of guilt. Especially, you Bradley, because you lost someone close to you and felt that you should've been here to help," Saffore stared at us from his chair as he jotted down some notes.

"I just don't understand why we didn't see this coming and why we couldn't get there in time? Why couldn't I absorb the bullets that shot my friend and everyone else? Why couldn't we speak to the different people to get them out of there? Why couldn't we talk the kid out of doing it? Why do people have to hate? Why couldn't we heal the wounded? Our family has all of these abilities that would've helped in that situation, and we missed it. We missed an opportunity to save eight people. We were somewhere laughing and having a good time, and they were dying," Bradley said, as we all stayed silent.

"Those are all great questions, Bradley. All of which I don't have the answer to. I can say that what you all have to battle here is bigger than skin, it's sin. Racism and hatred is not a skin issue, it's a sin issue. That fight is bigger than one person, a group of people, anything that we see. It's bigger than that," Saffore assured us.

"So it is a monster?" Allena asked. "Ali said last night that hatred is a monster. Is it?"

"In a way, yes it is, niecy-wiecy. Your family does have amazing abilities, but that doesn't mean you will save everyone or win every battle. This situation, even though it may hurt now, will make your family stronger. It will make your abilities stronger, and it will make your cause stronger. We do have a lot of crime, gun violence, and gang violence here in Chicago. Our Black communities need so much, but we also have to come together as a people. That means looking to the needs of others. I think your family can handle the needs of our Black community and help others as well. Kids I know you all may be in fear of what's going on, and I would recommend staying at home another week if you want. Take this advice. Don't allow this situation to change your heart, your purpose, or your outlook. Continue to want to help and save, and focus on helping and saving everyone you can. This fight is bigger than what you see. Let yourselves heal."

Saffore always knew exactly what to say to help our family and even though we weren't feeling it yet, this time was no different. He knew how to bring the spiritual side of things in to help us see a bigger picture. He understood our gifts and that we needed to be reminded that we were still human. This superhero thing isn't easy, but having some power is better than having no power at all.

CHAPTER 3 - PROMISES AND OATHS

"Students at John Lewis high school are coming back to school today. However, some students will stay home due to feelings of PTSD. We hope that all students get the help that they need, and more counselors have been provided to the school during this time. If anyone would like to attend our support groups we have many available. We have our PTSD support group. Anti-hatred support group. Anti-racism support group…"

These words came over the intercom from our assistant principal. Being back in school was a challenge. It's not the same place it used to be before the school shooting. I thought coming back after COVID19 was tense, but now everyone was apart because of sadness and fear, not sickness. Everyone was anxious and depressed, and many people were not present. The sound of all the support groups at school was still lingering over the intercom. Didn't adults realize that teenagers didn't want to talk about their problems to them? Being back was difficult for me because anytime someone hugged me, I felt more and more emotions. My best friend Zoe walked up to me but didn't hug me because she knew that I would feel everything she felt. Best friends are one part of what makes being a superhero easy. She knows that sometimes it's just better to tell me how she feels instead of getting close to me.

"You wanna eat lunch in an empty classroom today so we can talk about everything?" Zoe asked me.

"Yeah, that works. I kind of want to stay away from people anyway so that I don't touch them and they don't touch me. So I won't feel what everyone is feeling."

Bradley entered the building a few minutes after me. He stopped to talk to some of his teammates. He waved at Zoe, smirked at me, told us to have a good day, and put his hoodie back on. After Dad told him to take it off in the car. I thought I should say something, but I just didn't know what to say. I could tell my brother was sinking into that black hole I was dreaming about earlier. His eyes were down, his shoulders were slouched, and he didn't have the same swag that he used to. I understand losing Ahava was hard, but it's like he was second guessing everything.

"How is Bradley taking it?" Zoe asked me.

"Terribly. I held his hand the other day and…"

"Hi Alicia and Zoe, how are you two? Can I hug you?" Principal Westbrook came up to me and said.

"Sure," I said despite knowing I didn't want to be hugged. Why wasn't I just honest in telling her I didn't feel like it? She hugged Zoe and then me. As she hugged me for a long time, I could tell she felt sadness and fear. In her memories, I could see kids running out of the building and police officers outside. I guess she was reliving the day in her mind. Then I saw her seeing the kid who had committed the crime. I could only see the back of his head. No one told us who the shooter was. He had a mask on when he came in because of the pandemic. Of course the police department knew, but because he was a minor, no one had revealed his identity, yet.

"I know being here is hard, especially since one of the students we lost was a friend of your family's. We are here to support you and your family. Is your brother Bradley here today?" Principal Westbrook asked, still hugging me.

"Yes, he's here today," I responded, still in shock of her memories.

"Oh good, how is he?" She finally let go, but still held my shoulders.

"He hasn't been himself lately," I responded.

"Okay, I think he should sign up for one of our support groups. I think it would be good for him. You both have a good day, and let me know if you need anything." She finally walked away.

"Whoa," I said as she walked away.

"What happened? What did you see when she hugged you?" Zoe asked me.

"She was reliving the day the shooting happened."

"What was it like? I was out sick that day," Zoe said.

"Chaotic and scary, and she seemed to feel the same way, like she was having PTSD as well."

"How is it that you feel what all of these people feel all day and don't feel that way yourself?"

"Breathing and Blocking. There have been times I've been depressed and anxious, or gone into shock because of other people's feelings. But Uncle Saffore taught me to take a breath and let it go. Breathe in and Block it out. I mean, it helps to know what other people feel because I know what to say during a crime or when something happens. But I also have to block it out if there is nothing I can do about it. I better text Bradley that Westbrook will be coming his way."

"What were you saying you saw when you held Bradley's hand?" Zoe asked again.

"I'll tell you during lunch," I responded.

Bradley wasn't going to be too happy about this. He had hated talking directly about his anger lately. Especially with anyone at the school. You see, not very many people know about my family's abilities except for a few family members, the police chief, Saffore, Zoe, and my brother's friend who passed away. Our parents told us long ago not to tell anyone about it. So no one at school blamed us directly for not being there. They just thought we were lucky to be out of school during that time. But knowing that you can save people, especially those that you love, but you weren't there to save them was heartbreaking. My brother couldn't help feeling this, and I felt that if Principal Westbrook told him to join a support group, he may say something rude. I just decided to text him.

Principal Westbrook wants us to join a support group. I texted Bradley.

Why Bro, we didn't tell her we need anything? Bradley texted back.

I know, but just go. That way she doesn't have to tell you to go. She hugged me. I was able to see the shooter and felt a bunch of other things.

What did he look like? Bradley asked.

I only saw the back of his head. I assured him.

Oh. Okay.

So are you going to join?

Yeah, I'll just go to that anti-hate one. Good looking out.

You're welcome.

"Welcome to the anti-hate support group. I'm Mr. Thatcher, and since the tragic experience that your school has had, Principal Westbrook felt it necessary to have this talk. So if anyone would like to speak, we can. Please raise your hand and I'll hand you the talking stick."

Bradley hated being in the support group, but he felt that it was good to get some feelings out. While there, he met three guys he told me about, Kuzaliana, Chuki, and Taifa. He said they seemed pretty cool, so I was glad he was able to meet some new people that day. While he was in his support group, Zoe and I were eating lunch in an empty classroom. It was the most calm I'd felt for the past week. It was hard coming back to school and feeling safe after a school shooting. Bradley told me a bit about what he and the guys talked about.

"I can't believe they want us to sit in these support groups. How is something going to be anti-hate? Everyone hates," Chuki started out.

“Yeah, I mean this is so stupid. We don’t want to sit here and talk. Bradley, what do you think?” Taifa asked.

“Yeah, I don’t really want to be here either.” Bradley was confused as to why these guys were talking to him since he had never met them before. Since he’s pretty popular at school he thought maybe they knew him from baseball or coding, but he didn’t know them.

“Bro, I mean we don’t have to stay here if we don't want to. They wanted us to join, so we joined,” Kuzaliana said.

“Yeah, I guess you’re right?” Bradley looked at them, a bit confused.

“Sorry bro, I’m Chuki, that’s Taifa, and that’s Kuzaliana.”

“Oh, cool names,” Bradley said.

“Thanks. We’re about to head out, you wanna come?” Chuki asked.

“Sure, where y'all goin’?”

"Probably just sit in Chuki's car. I'mma smoke some kush," Taifa said.

"Oh, I don't smoke, bro," Bradley said.

"We don't either, only Taifa does. You good, he can stand outside the car," Chuki said. While I was sitting in the empty classroom, I saw Bradley out the window walking to the car with the guys. Taifa was standing outside to smoke, which was why I asked him about them. Him and Ahava didn't do that sort of thing, especially after Ahava worked hard to get clean when he turned his life around. Bradley told me he and the guys talked about the shooter while they were in the car.

"I don't understand. I mean, I hate the shooter for killing all those people. I hate the fact that we don't do anything to people for hating. I mean, we should have a hate group for those hateful people. Maybe that would keep them from doing things like that," Chuki kept going.

"Yeah, I wish someone could've come in and killed that kid. I mean, he killed himself anyway. That would've stopped him from killing all those people," Taifa said.

"Bradley, what do you think?" Kuzaliana asked.

"I mean, I don't know. I do hate the guy. He did kill my best friend. But he's gone now. What can we do about it?"

"Maybe we can start an anti-hate, hate group? That way if it happens again, we could stop it, and others can stop it," Kuzaliana said.

"I don't know, man. I would like to avenge my best friend's death. I wish justice could've been served, but the guy killed himself."

"Yeah, he did, but there are others out there like him. Besides, we know who did it," Chuki said.

"You do? Who did it?" Bradley asked.

"This kid named Razza. He has a friend that's planning on doing the shooting at his school. His name is Odio, and his high school is in Oak Park," Taifa said mid puff.

"How do you guys know this stuff?" Bradley asked.

"We have our sources. We need to stop this Odio guy. So Bradley, how you feel? I mean, how else can you avenge your friend's death? You couldn't stop his killer, so maybe you can stop the next guy," Kuzaliana asked.

"I mean, that would be good. We could save some more kids from dying, I guess."

"Let's make a pact or a promise that we stop these dudes from shooting other kids. By any means necessary. If no one else is going to serve justice, then we should," Taifa said.

"So how y'all gon' do this?" Bradley asked.

That day, before the four of them got back to class, they agreed that they would stop the shooter. They knew a few kids at the high school in Oak Park who could get them in. The next week, they used some other kids' school IDs to get into the school. Once in, just as planned, the kid Odio pulled out a gun. He shot a couple students. Chuki tackled him, and they started fighting the kid. Bradley helped Chuki fight, all the while wondering how these guys got so good at fighting. For a while, everything was going well. Many students were outside. Taifa and Kuzaliana helped the couple students who were wounded outside. Odio, still holding the gun, started to run. Chuki and Bradley chased after him. He started shooting at them, but they kept running and chasing. Soon they were outside, running towards an exit where no cops could be found. Odio stopped and began shooting at Chuki. Bradley jumped in front, and of course his body absorbed all three bullets. This is what he saw himself doing for his best friend, Ahava. The shooter was shocked and out of bullets. Chuki ran up to him and knocked him out cold. Bradley went up to them.

"Leave him here, we'll let the police find him. That way, justice can be served. We knew about your powers, Bradley. Ahava told us about you, and he knew you could help. Ahava got killed that day trying to stop the guy like you were trying to do. He would've been proud of you for helping. Let's go," Chuki said.

Because he was knocked out cold, the guy didn't remember much and just explained why he committed the crime to the police. He didn't remember much about Bradley, Chuki, Taifa, and Kuzaliana. There was also no camera footage in the area where they were, so no one caught anything. Lucky for Bradley because he was completely exposed that day. Everyone would've found out about him and our family. Even though I didn't like it, I loved seeing my brother happy again. But what bothered me was his actions. Our parents told us to never fight hatred with hatred. We also weren't supposed to be lying or hurting others. That wasn't our goal. But I guess it was for a good cause, right?

CHAPTER 4 - PERFECTION

Bradley had started spending a lot of time with the guys. He felt good having friends who knew his secret and who he connected with. I was happy for him, but also worried. They started stopping small hate crimes around the city. It's like Bradley had found a new family of superheroes to be a part of. We were out one night, my family and I. Bradley was supposed to be with us that night, but he was late. There had been some car-jackings at car dealerships, and the police had called us in to see if we could help out.

"Where is Bradley?" my dad asked in a hostile tone.

"He was hanging out with his friends," my mom responded.

"He's supposed to be here. I told him we had to take care of this tonight," my dad responded.

"He'll be here, Dad, Bradley wouldn't miss helping someone out," Wilson said. He looked up to Bradley.

"I'm here, so what's going on?" Bradley said, running up out of breath.

"Bradley, boy, why you late?" Dad asked in anger.

"I was with the crew, Dad. I lost track of time," Bradley responded.

"Last time I checked, we were your crew," Allena replied with an attitude.

"I'm sorry, I'll be on time next time," Bradley said. My dad just shook his head and cut his eyes at Bradley. Then told us the plan.

We went into the dealership, where the carjackers were already in the cars, getting ready to pull out of the dealership. There were about three divers and eleven guys in total. Calhoun stood in front of the parking lot exit. As the drivers drove towards the exit, Calhoun used his strength to stop three of the vehicles by holding his hands forward. It was an instant pile up. The airbags deployed. Because of the crash, the drivers were discombobulated. Calhoun removed them from the cars, and my dad took their guns. The other two cars were trying to leave from the other parking lot exit.

Calhoun held Lena's hand as she ran while the other carjackers were getting away. With lightning speed, she got Calhoun to the car, where Calhoun held on to the car and pulled it back. The carjackers tried shooting at them, but Bradley stood in front of them and absorbed all of the bullets. To the carjacker's surprise, my dad created a force field around the rest of us. My dad came up and pulled the boys out of the car, and both my parents knocked them out cold. The count was ten. Another guy was trying to get away, but Allena went up to him and pushed him down. He looked up at us, scared out of his mind. As we all stood above him in our metallic gray suits and masks, we saw how young and scared our carjackers were. The police came and handcuffed the eleven guys. All teenagers. Wilson healed their wounds while they were handcuffed.

I held on to one of their hands after they were cuffed. I told my parents, "They're scared and confused. They need help." My dad went over and talked to the chief. Many people didn't know this, but the chief knew my family's secret and would call us when certain problems, like car-jackings, were getting out of control. We would come in and help out. No one knew but the chief because the chief and my dad had been high school friends. He knew he could call the Splendid Saba when the department needed some help. He would act as if they got the call after we stopped the crime and show up just in time to discuss things with my dad.

"Look, they're just kids," my dad told the chief.

"Sylvester, you know these kids have to pay for this crime," the chief responded.

"My wife and I can help them. I'll represent them in court. I already know everything that happened because I was here. We'll have them do some community service at our center so we can help them. They look no more than 16. You know we can help them."

"Okay, but you can't save everyone, Sylvester. I'll talk to the judge next week to see what we can do."

My mom and dad believed in justice, but they also believed in loving all people and helping those in need. They believed that in order to correct crimes committed, we had to help the individuals committing the crime. They never wanted to hurt anyone physically or mentally. If possible, they wanted to help them to not commit crimes again by giving them a second chance to make things right. This is why they'll have Wilson heal wounds, my dad will represent them in court, they'll have them come to the community center to get help, and our goal is to never kill people. I can't even tell you how many kids went back to school and graduated instead of turning back to a life of crime just because my parents wanted to help them out. Of course, I looked at my mother and father like they were perfect, but all of my siblings didn't. When we got home that night, Bradley had a lot to say. Once my dad pulled into our garage, Bradley jumped out of the car first. My dad followed behind him as he went into the house. My mom jumped out of the car after, followed by me and the rest of my siblings. We knew there would be a big argument since Bradley was late.

"Bradley, we're not finished. I don't know if I like you spending so much time with those new friends of yours," my dad said, as he and Bradley entered the house.

"Pops, I was late," Bradley responded, annoyed. "I said I was sorry."

"You've been late a lot. You haven't been at home a lot. I understand you miss Ahava and you're trying to get past what happened, but Son, you can't shut us out."

“Pops, you don’t understand me. Only Alicia and Mom truly do because of their powers. You’re only focused on what you want us to do.”

“Watch your mouth when you talk to me, boy.”

“You want to help and save everyone, but not everyone can be helped, Dad.”

“This is not what we believe…”

“This dude killed my best friend, and I wasn’t there to save him. I couldn’t do anything about it, and you want me to forgive him? And if we were there, were we supposed to help him while he tried to kill Ahava?”

“This is what we believe…”

“Maybe that’s not what I believe. You want to choose the battles we fight, but there are other battles. I don’t have to fight every battle just with y'all. There are other people I can save. My crew knows about my powers, and we stop hate crimes. We stopped a school shooting at a school in Oak Park. Maybe this is what I want to do.”

"You told someone your secret and went to another school and stopped a shooter?"

"I don't know why I expected you to understand," Bradley asked as he turned and walked away.

"Don't you turn around when I'm talking to you. You want to talk real tough and be with your crew. You should go stay with your crew then."

"SYLVESTER…" my mom yelled after she sensed the conversation was getting heated. The rest of us just stood at the door watching the action. Part of me felt bad for Bradley, he was just trying to find his way after losing his best friend. I felt bad for my parents too, they just wanted to keep the family together. None of us knew what else to say, we just stood watching my dad and brother argue.

"No, no, he has all the answers, why doesn't he go?" my dad said. "I'm not going to be disrespected in my house Viv. I pay for this house."

"I pay for this house as well, and you're not putting our son out. Sylvester, how can you want to help other people's kids when you're not trying to help your own son? He's hurting!"

"Naw, Ma, it's cool if he doesn't want me here I don't have to be here," Bradley responded.

"Bradley, no, we want you here. Everyone just needs some time and rest. We had a long night," my mom stood between my brother and my dad.

Everyone listened to my mom that night and headed to bed, but I'm sure my parents had the argument of the century. I didn't hear anything, so I guess that meant my dad placed a forcefield around their bedroom while they argued. Bradley texted me and told me that he was going out to be with the guys. They needed him to help them out because some kids were tagging a Muslim family's house with racist paraphernalia Bradley went out that night and didn't come home the next morning. My parents were looking for him.

When they called his cell phone, he didn't answer. That morning, I told them what happened. I told them what he texted me, about the guys, their names, and my dream. We all got dressed so we could go find Bradley. My dad went to our school and told the principal the kids' names, and she said no students attended this school with those names. We contacted the chief of police to see if he knew their names, but he told us that they didn't have their names in the system. They did have camera footage with Chuki's license plate number after I told them what the car looked like. We were able to find the car and track it.

I didn't have to touch my parent's hand to know how worried they were about Bradley. I told my mom and dad not to worry, and that we'd find Bradley.

"So there is a hate group rally happening, and y'all want to go down there, and y'all want me to kill some of the people?" Bradley asked the guys as they all were standing inside of an old abandoned home's garage.

"Yeah, Bradley. That way we can make an example out of these guys. They're spreading hatred. So in order to stop it, we have to show people that it's not okay, and we won't tolerate it." Chuki said.

"Y'all, I didn't sign up to kill anyone. That's not what we said…"

"We said by any means necessary. That's what you promised. I know you can absorb bullets, but can't you, like, shoot them out too?" Taifa assumed.

"I don't know, I never used my powers to shoot anyone, just to absorb the bullets. I've never tried. Bullets kill people, and I don't kill people…"

"Well, we do. And don't think you gon' leave this. We're just like you. Don't think you're so special. That those superhuman powers you got can't be stopped. Ahava didn't tell us about you. We've been watching you. We know what you can do and what you're capable of. Kuzaliana, Taifa, and I have been here for centuries. We just take on different forms. You see, Bradley, our whole focus is hatred. There is no fighting hatred with hatred. It only creates more hatred. You thought you were doing a good deed, but you were just hatin'. We have been spewing hatred long before there was racism, long before there was race, long before you. As long as we're here, it's not going to stop. You humans attach racism to a person. It's not a person. It's a…"

"It's a sin issue, a monster, a demon, a…"

"Yeah, we've been called all of those things. Who do you think was there with Hitler, Mussolini, and Hirohito? We're always seeking who we can devour. Whenever we're present, hatred comes…"

"STAY AWAY FROM MY SON," my dad yelled as we all barged in. We were finally at the abandoned house where they were staying, ready to save my brother.

Just then, as they saw my dad barging in, they pushed Bradley aside. Of course, they knew he couldn't be hurt, so there was no point in trying to hurt him. So they just had to fight. But with the Stantons you don't just fight one of us, you fight all of us. Bradley had a smile on his face when he saw us. This was the first time I had seen him smile since Ahava died. When you're a prodigal son and your family comes to save you, I guess it feels pretty good.

The three men, Chuki, Taifa, and Kuzaliana, stood together to fight us. My parents took on Chuki. Bradley and I took on Taifa. The twins and Lena took on Kuzaliana. After much fighting the guys did something we had never seen before. They combined into one huge monster that was bigger and stronger than any of us. This monster kept changing color, but not just any color — flesh colors. Its clothes turned into the word hatred in many different languages. This word seemed to be tattooed on these many flesh toned colors. Its voice said nothing but hateful things.

“Bradley, what are these guys?” my mom asked as they were turning into the monster.

“It’s just like Alicia said, Ma, they’ve been around for centuries,” Bradley said. “They’re not human, they're monsters.”

“Wait, Bradley, what are their names again?” Wilson asked.

“Their names were Chuki, Taifa, and Kuzaliana,” Bradley responded.

“Guys, those names are Swahili for hatred, nation, and breed,” Wilson told us.

“Whatchu tryin’ to say, Wil?” Calhoun asked.

“Their names in a way stand for racism or racial hatred. So technically, we’re fighting racism. Why do you think no one else knew about them? Why do you think they came to Bradley? He was in a bad place, and he has his gifts.”.

“So what do we do? Our ancestors didn’t fight racism like this,” Calhoun asked.

"All that we can do. Be splendid," my dad said.

My family fought the monster. We don't kill people, but we don't mind killing monsters. Of course, we didn't kill the monster that day. After all the fighting we could accomplish, we tired it out. Before it flew away, it said, "This ain't over because I ain't over." As splendid as my family may be, killing racism is a collective effort that takes all people. But whenever it shows up again, we'll be there. At least my brother Bradley is back with us, and he realized that you can't fight hatred with hatred. Because of that, no more school shootings happened in Chicago. I guess the monster knew we were there and stayed away. Once we thought about it, our school shooting did happen when we weren't present as well. And the monster did try to split our family up by getting close to Bradley. I guess the Splendid Saba isn't a group you want to mess with.

CHAPTER 5 - EXONERATION

“So we can see and fight monsters now, huh? What can’t we do?” Wilson said as we walked out of the abandoned house to our car.

“Break apart. Pops, I’m sorry for everything that I did. I couldn’t believe I was so stupid,” Bradley said to my dad.

“Son you weren’t stupid,” my dad said. “You were hurt, and instead of making you fight for my causes I should’ve understood that you missed Ahava. Being a superhero can be tough. We don’t have all of the answers even though we’re expected to. I’m sorry I wasn’t there for you.”

“You do know those guys will be back.” my mom said.

"Yeah but we'll be ready, Ma!" Calhoun smiled at my mom.

"Right, maybe this is why we are the way we are. Maybe we can fight for our people and all people," Wilson walked up to Calhoun and my mom.

"Like Uncle Saffore said. Because all people are deserving of love, right Mama?" Asked Allena. I was holding her hand as we walked out of the storage garage. Holding her hand was always the best. Her feelings were always happy, playful, and joyful. Because she knows that I can tell what she's feeling and see her memories she would always bring to remembrance hugging me and mouthing that she loved me.

"That's right, baby. That's what God is and that's why Jesus died for us."

My family may be dysfunctional, crazy, obnoxious — need I go on? But they are also loving, talented, creative, helpful, and utterly splendid. Our work doesn't stop here though. As long as there is crime and corruption in Chicago (I think all three of those words are synonymous) we'll always be here to try and stop it. And as long as there is hatred in this world, we'll always be here to stop it.

Ring. Ring. Ring.

The next day a call was coming on our superhero line. It was the police chief. My dad was out for a run, while my mom was at the university, and my siblings and I were at school.

"Sylvester, how is everything? Did you all find Bradley?" the chief asked.

"Yeah Chief, we found him," my dad said. "He's okay."

"Great, glad to hear it. I have a question for you and your family."

"We just got finished with a little scuffle to get Bradley back, we're a bit tired. What is it, Chief? Another carjacking?"

“No, something much bigger?”

“What?”

“Gun violence. What can you do about it?”

PART 2: DADDY ISSUES

CHAPTER 1: FAMILY MAN

"Your honor, my clients are just children. I'm asking today for you to not charge them as adults for the carjacking. No one was hurt and no cars were stolen."

"Well that's because Chicago's real heroes were there to stop them. How do you think they would feel if we just let these kids go free?" How did this judge know how my family felt? I wished I could knock him out right now. These are the moments when I wish I could tell our secrets. I wish that I could reveal to the world who my family is and that we're the Splendid Saba. And what did he mean by Chicago's real heroes?

“Your honor with all due respect, if the heroes are not here, I don’t think we can understand how they might feel. But what I did see from the footage is that they did not want to hurt these children. They healed them, they stopped them, and turned them over to the police. I am asking if they can do house arrest and community service at my youth center with my wife and I. That way, they may receive their education while getting tutoring and counseling from us at the center. Isn’t the judicial system supposed to correct your honor? Then allow me to help in that correction. If these children are tried as adults for this crime, they’re looking at a longer sentence. Possibly a life headed towards more crime and more sentencing. Haven’t we all done something we regret as teenagers? Weren’t you ever given a second chance?”

“Sylvester, it is only because of your track record with helping Chicago’s youth that I will even allow this. But if any child you defend ever commits a crime again, no matter how big or small, I will never allow this again in my courtroom. That means any other child you represent after that, I will convict them for their crime and they will be tried as an adult in my courtroom. Do you understand?" The judge asserted.

"Clearly, your honor."

"You can't save them all, Sylvester. Some are just bad seeds." With a bang of his gavel, the case was over. Another court case won.

Another successful day on the job. The kids that my family and I caught carjacking the dealership stood trial today. Every time I looked those kids in the eyes, I saw my own. If I did not have what I have — the gifts I have, the career I have — I would want someone to do the same for my kids. Whenever I walk out of the courthouse, like I did today, I always think about my own Black children. Being a father was the best and most important job that I had. My family was what kept me going. I always worried if I was doing the right thing by allowing my children to fight crime alongside my wife and I. They seemed to love it, but I knew the pressure got to them.

Bradley was starting to open up more and smile more since Ahava's passing, but I could tell he still blamed himself for not being there to protect him during the school shooting. Alicia was still unsure of who she was, what she wanted to do, and how she really felt. Calhoun recently had another sickle cell crisis and had to go to the hospital. The boys were at school, so the school rushed him to the hospital. Of course, Wilson was able to heal him, but their teachers don't know that. I was glad we did go to the hospital because Wilson walked into a few rooms, talking to kids and healing them with his gift. I told that boy not to go around doing that without people's permission. But I guess it was good practice since he wanted to be a doctor one day. Calhoun was back being his strong, crazy self once we left the hospital. And my baby girl, well, she's just as smart, quick, and sassy as ever.

I loved my kids. They were the most wonderful kids I could ever ask for, gifts, flaws, and all. But I had a feeling that they were not always honest with me about how they felt. Were they afraid to tell me how they felt? Did they think it was because of me that we had to be Splendid Saba? Being a father has been the hardest job I've ever had to do. I'd never gotten down on my knees and prayed so much until the day I became a father.

Ring. Ring. Ring. That was the superhero line. I drove from the courthouse to pick up some Giordano's pizza, which I always did when I had something important to talk to my family about.

"Sly here." I said.

"Sylvester, so what do you say about tackling the gun violence issue?" The chief said abruptly on the other end of the superhero line. Did he think I didn't have a life outside of being the leader of Splendid Saba?

"Hey Chief, I'm fine, and you? How was work today?"

"I get it, I get it. Hi, Sly."

"Thank you. I knew you could be cordial, Chief. I gotta talk to the family about it tonight. But it's funny, you as the police chief are talking to me about stopping gun violence in Chicago."

"Why is that funny? I feel that you and your family can handle it. It's too big of a problem for the CPD."

"I'm not saying that my family can't handle it. You wouldn't believe the monster we just recently fought. But if I'm being honest, my kids and my wife are tired of the gun violence in Chicago. But you know what they're going to ask me, Chief."

"What?"

"They're going to talk about police brutality as well. That's still gun violence, Chief."

"I know, and I can't ask you to fight against the gang and gun violence when there are those who do the same in my police department. What if some of you tackle the gang and gun violence and the others get down to what's going on in the CPD? I mean we've tried changing our training, talking about this issue, talking about Blue Lives Matter and Black Lives Matter and what that all means. I mean, I'm a Black man and a police chief myself so I carry both identities."

"Chief, you know people have to change their thoughts before they change their actions. Look, it sounds like a plan to me, but you know I have to ask the family first. I'll call you tonight. I'll stop and grab some Giordano's. Maybe that'll lighten the delivery."

"Do whatchu gotta do, Sly. I'll call you back around 9:00 tonight."

Fighting against gun violence was a big step for my kids. My wife and I grew up hearing gunshots all the time.

Seeing people killed in our communities often. Whether at the hands of other Black people or the police. I never thought I'd be asked if my family could do something about it. As I walked into Giordano's, I processed over and over how I would break the news to my wife and kids.

"Sly whatchu doing here, boy? How you doin?" Ernie, the pizza guy at Giordano's asked me.

"I'm good, Ernie! How you doin', man?" I asked him, smiling underneath my pandemic mask.

"I can't complain. You comin' to get yo kids some pizza?"

"Yeah, I gotta make a big announcement to them tonight. Wanna use the pizza to soften the delivery."

"Aw naw, yo wife ain't pregnant again, is she? Y'all got enough kids as it is."

"Why you so focused on my wife man?"

"Sly, yo wife is fine, man. I don't know why she witchu." I couldn't argue with him, my wife was fine. "If she ever drop you, you know Imma be right there to console her."

"Aye, stay away from my wife, man. Especially if we break up."

"But them kids, they goin' witchu. I ain't takin' care of all them kids. I don't care how fine she is. Let me get that pizza ready man."

"Yeah, you do that." Ernie was a funny old man that I knew from my old neighborhood. He'd worked at Giordano's for a long time, and I always come to his spot to get my pizza. He never knew about my gifts, but he'd always been like an uncle to me. No matter how much he loved my wife. Ernie was an older guy who looked out for me as a kid. I lost my dad when I was younger, around eight. He died from cancer, and Ernie was one of the older guys from the neighborhood who looked out for me. He helped raise me and wanted me to go down the right path. He made a difference in my life, and that's why I try to do that for other children.

While waiting for Ernie, I ran outside. There was a car accident, and a woman and her baby had gotten hit while they were in their car. I could see that they were fine, but other cars and trucks were coming. There was about to be a big car pile-up on the Kennedy Expressway. Just after the 18 wheeler hit another car, it started to spiral. It almost hit a guy on a motorcycle. Before this car crushed this motorcycle driver I used my force field to stop the car from spiraling into it. A second car came towards the car I stopped, so I created a force field around that one. More and more were coming. Didn't these people see a car in the middle of the road? I created force fields around eight other cars. I put the first car off to the shoulder. After so much honking and cursing, I decided to remove the force fields. Road rage is a mug. The cars were all on their way now. I put the car with the woman and her baby on the shoulder as well so they can calm down. Hopefully no one noticed me using my forcefields. I tried to be careful so no one would see me, so I used the confusion of the accidents to duck back into the restaurant.

"Alright, Sly," Ernie said as he startled me.

"What?"

"Here is your pizza man, remember?"

"Oh yeah, alright Ernie."

"You tell that wife of yours I said hello."

"I won't."

On my way back home, of course not on the Kennedy expressway, the chief texted me a photo of all of the cars moving along on the shoulders of the expressway. Under the photo he said, "This looks like your work." I didn't respond. Back at home, my wife knew something was up as soon as I brought home Giordano's.

"I was just about to cook," she said, looking fine as ever standing in the kitchen of our home.

"Well no need to, Ernie cooked it," I responded.

"How is Ernie?"

"Good, thinking about you." My wife had a huge smile on her face. "Stop smiling."

"What? Ernie is a sweet man. So why do we need pizza tonight? What do you have to tell us?"

"A man can't bring his family some deep dish pizza without there being a problem?" I asked as I pulled my wife close. I didn't know if it was her being intuitive or just knowing me all too well. Either way, I loved this woman. She was what held our family together in so many rough times. This gorgeous Black woman who was smart, sophisticated, elegant, and amazing. She is Maya Angelou, Michelle Obama, and Gabrielle Union all rolled into one.

"A man can, but not you," she responded looking me in the eyes.

"I do have something to ask you and the kids. I thought the pizza would soften you up."

"Did you bring dessert?"

"I stopped at Garret's Popcorn on the way home."

"Then I'm softened."

"Bro, I smell Giordano's." Calhoun, Bradley, and Wilson all came charging down the stairs and into the kitchen along with cousin Jamal. I'm sure after playing NBA 2k or Fortnite since they got home from school. I should've gotten two more pizzas. I thought three would be enough, but I forgot these boys be hungry like hostages. You would think we didn't feed them.

"Wash your hands, bro, and get the plates out for everyone. Where are my girls?" I asked.

"Alicia is in her room with Zoe writing and doing homework of course. And Allena is playing with her L.O.L. dolls with cousin Jael. She sped through her homework," Calhoun responded, staring at the pizza boxes.

“I’ll go grab them.” My wife sashayed away.

“So Pops, what’s the pizza for?” Bradley asked me. My kids too? This family has no faith in me.

“Can’t a father buy his family some Giordano’s?” I asked.

“C’mon Pops, you know when you really want to do something nice for us, you’ll take us to Giordano’s. But when you have something to tell us, you bring Giordano’s home. I’m fine with it either way, I’m starved.” Bradley said. He was right, I did do that sometimes. It doesn’t feel good when your son calls you out like that.

“Just wait for your mom, sisters, and Jael to get back,” I assured them.

“Wait a minute, Bradley, he brought popcorn too,” Wilson chimed in.

“Aw naw, Pops — wait is mama pregnant again?” Bradley whined as they all sat at our breakfast table in the kitchen. Why did everyone think my wife was pregnant?

“Dad, Splendid Saba isn’t going to sound good if there are eight of us,” Wilson interjected. They all started laughing at me.

“Aye y'all, be cool, okay? I’ll tell you what my announcement is after we eat dinner,” I said. I couldn’t stand these kids.

Giordano’s boxes were left crust-less. Jael and Jamal had gone home, but Zoe was still there. My family was laid out on our sofa eating Garrett’s popcorn. Now was the time for me to pop the question. Why hadn’t Zoe gone?

“Uh, Zoe, you don’t have to be home?” I asked her.

“No, my mom told me I can stay with you guys if I want,” she said as she kept eating her popcorn.

“Zoe, my dad has something really important to tell us, so I’ll tell you about it later,” Alicia said.

"Oh, gotcha. I'll see you tomorrow then," Zoe said as she got up to leave. Finally I could tell them what had been on my mind all day.

"So Daddy what's wrong?" Alicia asked. She knew when she asked I would just come out and say it. I don't know why every dad has a soft spot for their daughters. She just asked so politely, unlike my sons. For some reason, I felt like she already knew what I was going to ask.

"Well Bay Bay," that's what I called her, "All y'all, the chief came to me and asked me if we could fight a bigger crime. Bigger than what we've ever fought before."

"What is it?" my wife asked. I could tell by her face she wasn't excited.

"I mean, the car-jackings are down now. No more school shootings or big hate crimes have happened. What's next?" Calhoun asked. I paused for a minute before I gave my big announcement.

"Daddy, is it gun violence?" Alicia asked. She did hug me before dinner, so maybe she saw.

"How did you know that?" I asked her.

"I saw it when I hugged you before dinner," Alicia responded. See what I mean?

"That's it, don't hug me anymore when I bring Giordano's home." I wasn't serious, I loved my Bay Bay's hugs. They brought me joy. She just rolled her eyes.

"Pops, the chief asked you to ask us to fight against gun violence," Bradley said. "Does he know we fought against a racial hatred monster a few months ago?"

"No Bradley, he doesn't really know what we fought against," I said. "And he didn't ask."

"So Dad, the question that I had all night was if we're fighting against gun violence, how are we doing it?" Alicia asked. "Is it just the gun violence in Black and Brown neighborhoods, or is it also the brutality from the police?" Oh Alicia, she was lucky she was my favorite after Allena.

"It's both. You should know," I said to her sarcastically, but she just smiled.

"Cool, I was gon' say we can't fight against one without the other," Wilson said.

"Sylvester, I don't know how I feel about this," my wife said. I knew I should've brought home more popcorn.

"What's wrong, Ma?" Alicia asked her mother as she reached for her hand.

"Alicia, you don't have to hold my hand, I'm capable of explaining how I feel," my wife said. "This is a big task. It's not like the kids can't get hurt. Well, one of them can't and one of them has healing gifts, but the others are vulnerable. How are we going to fight against both?"

"Well, I had the idea of maybe splitting the job," I had to say it had been my idea because if I said it was the chief's idea my wife would block him from the super hero line. "You know I can temporarily use Bradley and Wilson's gifts, so I can take Calhoun and Allena with me, and you can take Bradley, Wilson, and Alicia with you. We could get some answers from the neighborhood, and y'all could get some answers inside the CPD."

"That's your plan, to split us up?" My wife wasn't havin' it.

"Well I thought we could fight both simultaneously," I responded.

"You need to do some more thinking because I ain't happy with this plan," my wife folded her arms and gave me that look that she always gives when she's mad at me.

"C'mon, our family fought against racial hatred a few months back," I tried to convince her as my kids sat on the couch staring at us. "If we can do that, we can fight against gun violence."

"Daddy, but we didn't win. The monster will be back," Allena said.

"I know that, baby, but we tried, and we did that to help your brother. So think about this, it helps so many people if we do this. If one of our kids was in the middle of this, we would want to help them," I responded to my baby girl.

"I know, but I feel like something is going to happen. Something bad," my wife said afraid.

"And it might, but look, I thought about this," I assured her. "You can go to the CPD because that's a more complex system. You'll be able to figure it out easily. We'll do the streets because we know some of the kids that we've helped will talk."

"Kids, how do y'all feel?" my wife asked.

"We're okay, Mama," Alicia said.

"Yeah I'm fine with it, I think splitting up for a bit will be okay," Calhoun stated after.

"I'm fine as long as we get to help people," Allena smiled and Wilson nodded.

"Bradley?" my wife asked. My oldest son was still quiet.

“Ma, do you think when I absorb bullets, I can shoot them out?” Everyone paused after Bradley asked this question.

“That’s random,” Alicia said.

“I know, but the monster said something along those lines before you guys came,” Bradley explained. “It’s been in my head ever since. And now that we’re talking about gun violence, I want to know. I don’t want to be a walking gun myself.”

“What are you worried about, Bradley?” I asked my son. I could see the fear in his eyes.

“I guess I just wanna know. If someone tries to hurt Mama, or Ali, or Wil, I don’t know how I might react. And Pops, you’re usually there. You come up with the plan, so I don’t feel as much responsibility. But I won’t allow anybody to hurt them, so there is no telling what I might do.”

“If this has been bothering you, Bradley, why didn’t you tell us?” my wife asked.

“It didn’t bother me as much until now. It’s not that I don’t want to do it, but I just think we should visit Uncle Saff first. Just so I’ll know for sure,” Bradley told us holding his head down.

“We can do that, Son. But besides that, everyone is on board?” I asked.

“Not everyone.” My wife wouldn’t budge.

“What’s wrong now, Viv…?” I asked her before I was interrupted.

“Another little girl was shot tonight on the West Side of Chicago. This time she was only seven years old and a stray bullet intended for another target hit her in the chest. She is at Stroger Hospital in critical condition. Her family is here, wondering where it all went wrong. Her mother had this to say…” Allena had turned on the local news. My baby was a genius. I guess it was just what my wife needed to get on board.

"Mama, we have to do something so we can help all the little kids like me. They shouldn't have to die." After Allena said this, a pause came over the room as we waited for my wife's response. Matthew 21:16 says, "Out of the mouth of babe's and nursing infants You have perfected praise."

"Okay, we can do it," my wife said after heaving a big sigh. I guess that was all she needed to hear to agree to the mission.

"I know we can," I assured her.

Ring. Ring. Ring. It had just made 9:00 pm and the chief was calling.

"Yeah Chief, we're splendid."

CHAPTER 2 · BENJAMIN

The next day, I took Bradley to see Saffore. My wife thought it best if he and I went to see Saffore as she didn't know how she would be able to handle it if our son was a human weapon. She also wanted us to go so he and I could talk a bit more. Ever since his blow up after Ahava died, she thought it best for us to spend more time together. I could tell my son had been dealing with a lot since Ahava's passing. Being a young Black boy in America, but especially Chicago, was already tough. Then to be a superhero with gifts you don't understand is an added headache. Then your best friend just got shot, and you can absorb bullets, but you weren't there to save him. My son was dealing with a lot. I knew Bradley may not understand, but his superpower was one thing that gave me peace. With living in Chicago and now fighting against gun violence, you don't understand how much it had crossed my mind that my 16-year-old Black son was bullet proof. Imagine how many mothers and fathers wished the same for their kids, especially their Black sons. Whether he can shoot bullets or not didn't bother me. I was just glad that he couldn't get hurt. Even though he'd been a bit distant lately, Bradley was my ace. He was the most like me in spirit. I named him Benjamin for his middle name. In the Bible, that means "son of my right hand." I was happy to have a son and always knew that he'd be my right hand man in life, and in our superhero life. It would be odd not fighting alongside him for this mission.

"So Bradley, how you feelin'?" I asked him as we drove to Saffore's lab.

“I don’t know, Pops, a bit worried and anxious, and if I can shoot bullets, I want to learn how to control it. You know I never want to hurt anybody, just help.”

“I know, Son, and whatever happens, whether you can shoot bullets or not, we'll find a way for you to use your gift to not hurt anyone. Your mother, Saffore, and I will help you to control it.”

“Yeah I know, Pops.”

“Son, how long have you been feeling like this?”

“I guess it’s been off and on since we fought the racial hatred monster a couple weeks back. They asked me if I could shoot bullets since I can absorb them. And it’s just been on my mind. Can I actually do that? And I’ve never needed to do that or had to do it. But when you told us about the gun violence mission and me going with Mama, Ali, and Wilson, I felt that maybe I should try it. I don’t want to just accidentally shoot someone one day trying to protect all of us.”

"You know, you said something about me always being responsible for our family, but that is very responsible of you. I'm proud of you, Son. I'm proud of the brilliant young man you are, the man you're becoming, and the man you will be."

"Thanks, Pops."

We pulled up to Saffore's lab. As always, my homie was in good spirits.

"My brotha, how you been?" Saff smiled at me.

"I'm good, Saff," I grabbed his hand and pulled him in for a hug.

"Nephew, what's good?" Saff asked Bradley.

"I'm good, Unc, just wondering if you can tell me about any extra gifts, I guess," Bradley fist bumped Saff.

Once inside his lab, Saffore ran a multitude of tests on Bradley. I was glad to have someone close to our family who knew so much about science. For a while, he had Bradley in a bullet proof chamber, and it looked as if he was playing some type of virtual reality game.

"Now Nephew, this isn't going to be some regular virtual reality game. It'll be your worst fears popping up. If you can shoot bullets, the room you're inside is bulletproof, fireproof, and water resistant. It would take me opening the door to let you out. Your father and I can see you. Wear these goggles, and we'll see what you're capable of," Saffore told Bradley.

"Are you ready, Son?" I asked.

"Yeah Pops, I think so," Bradley didn't look concerned, but I don't think he knew exactly what was to come.

"So what do you think, Saff?" I asked.

"You know, I always thought if he can absorb bullets because his skeleton is made of steel, he could possibly shoot them," Saff responded. "I never saw where the bullets actually went once they entered his body. Also, we've never shot at him. I mean, you're not going to shoot your own son, and I'm not going to shoot my nephew. So who knows where the bullets go when they enter him. I don't know if he can or can't shoot from his body. If he can, keep him close, Sly. He's the human weapon that so many people want fighting in their armies."

"But Saff, you know my son isn't like that."

"I know. Bradley is a good kid, but I see how this superhero thing gets to you all. Especially you and him."

"You noticed, huh?"

"Yes, he wants to be just like you, so he puts his heart and soul into this. Just as you do. And I know you don't want it to hurt him or the rest of your family."

"Saff, I've always meant to ask you. How come you never drank the elixir? You know, so you can have gifts like us."

"How do you think I became such a great scientist, psychologist, pastor, and therapist?"

"What? Saff, you've always been a great scientist. You were Saffore Urkel in college. The Morehouse Steve Urkel."

"Yeah, I remember. I was good, Sly, but not this good. I guess God gives us the gifts He feels are beneficial to us. So after drinking the elixir I thought maybe I'd be super strong like Calhoun, super speedy like Lena, or a healer like Wilson. But no, I became smarter, and that helped me to become an amazing scientist. I am a little like Alicia though, but she's better."

"So you know what someone is feeling?"

"They call it interpersonal and intrapersonal intelligence. This is heightened as well. So I'm superhuman like you all. That's what makes me a good pastor, psychologist, and therapist. I'm glad that these are my gifts because your family needs a lot of help from me as a scientist, therapist, pastor, brother, and uncle. And I feel that it is my fault that you all are like this."

"Don't blame yourself, Saff, nothing is your fault. And without you, we wouldn't be able to get through this. We wouldn't understand our gifts or be able to handle everything mentally and spiritually."

"I guess."

"Hey, why isn't Bradley doing anything?" I began to ask.

"I haven't turned the meter all the way up," Saffore asked. "The meter goes all the way up to ten, and once it's at ten his worst fears may start to pop up in his mind. The meter is only at three. I turn it up every couple of minutes. Right now he may just be experiencing not winning a baseball game or asking his crush out and her saying no."

"Wait, you know who his crush is?"

"No, but Ali might."

"True."

"Sly, when we turn it all the way up to ten Bradley may see something really dark. I don't know how he'll respond. But it's the only way for me to see his reaction."

"Will it hurt him?"

"Not physically, of course, but I don't know how he may feel."

"Okay, do what you need to do."

I didn't know what Bradley was seeing inside his virtual reality worst fears. I didn't want my son to go back to being withdrawn, but I wanted him to find out what he could do. Saffore turned the meter up to eight, and I saw my son fight harder than I had ever seen him fight before. Of course, Bradley was bumping into the walls. He couldn't get hurt, so him bumping into walls wasn't a problem. It was him being mentally hurt. I also saw Bradley's steel skeleton show through his skin. It was odd seeing my son's skin just fade away as he turned into steel. He was moving around the room, still bumping into the walls, fighting and kicking.

"Saff, he seems like he's really going through it. I think we should stop."

"Sly, I can't stop. He wants to know. The meter is only at eight."

Saff turned the meter up to nine. Bradley started screaming and punching the walls. Jumping off the walls. Kicking and screaming more.

"Saff, stop, I don't think this is a good idea."

"I can't, Sly, he wants to know."

He turned it up to ten. Bradley screamed. We heard twenty-seven gun shots and saw bullets coming out of my son. Then he fell to the floor on his knees and breathed heavily.

"TURN IT OFF, SAFFORE," I yelled as I ran to the door. "OPEN THE DOOR." Saff had turned off the machine and started to unlock the door so I could get in.

"Wait, Sly, as you go in, make yourself bulletproof. You don't know how Bradley will react."

"I don't care, that's my son." I walked into the chamber. Bradley's hands were clenched into fists. I touched his shoulders and pulled off his virtual reality mask. He was crying and still breathing hard. I made myself bulletproof. As I picked him up to place him on his feet, he pushed my hand away. Sure enough, he shot at me five times. It didn't hurt me, though. I couldn't absorb bullets like my son, but it just bounced off of me.

"I'm here, Son. I'm here, what happened?" He was still crying and breathing hard and mumbled something.

"I couldn't save you. I'm sorry Pops, I couldn't save you."

"I'm here, Son. I'm here." He was still crying and breathing hard as I held him close and hugged him. He didn't hug me back for a minute. Then his eyes seemed to open.

"Pops?"

"Yeah Son, I'm here, it's okay. I'm here." I looked him in his eyes. "Tell me what happened." He started to wipe his eyes.

"Sly, look at this." Saffore called me. I turned around and saw bullet dents in the wall but no bullets on the floor. He ran out to view the camera footage. He slowed it down.

"Sly, Bradley, does shoot bullets but it seems as if they absorb right back into him. So the bullets come out of him, and then like a boomerang or magnet, they come right back to him. So they're a part of him. He doesn't have to reload."

"Did you hear that, Bradley?"

Bradley stood there just looking down at the floor. Then he said,

"Pops, I couldn't save us."

On the car ride home Bradley was quiet. I didn't want my son going back to the dark place he was in a couple months ago, so I decided to talk to him about what he saw.

“Bradley, tell me what you saw in there?”

“First, things were fine. I couldn’t hit a few baseballs. I didn't have a date for prom. Stuff like that. Then I saw Ahava. He was alive again, but he was mad at me for not saving him. He shot you since I didn’t save him. He killed you. I held you in my arms, lifeless. Then the next thing I know, we were battling the racial hatred monster again without you. Everyone was looking to me to lead them. Then we started fighting, and everyone died and I couldn’t save them,” Bradley told me.

I stopped the car and pulled over. I told Bradley to get out of the car. Then I stepped out of the car and over to his side and hugged my son.

“Son, Ahava’s death was not your fault. You can’t keep feeling that it is.” He started crying again. “And you’re not here to protect me, I’m here to protect you. That’s what a father does. I’m here for you, and don’t worry about protecting the whole family. That's my job. And if you're not ready to do this mission, we don't have to…"

"DAD, WATCH OUT." Just then, a car slammed right into another car that was in front of it, pushing it right towards us. I put a forcefield around us to make us invisible so no one would see us, record it, and post it. It was hard being a secret superhero when there were cameras, camera phones, and social media everywhere. The car flipped over a couple times. I put a force field around the car and landed it on the ground, wheels down. I took the force field off of us, and we got back in the car.

"C'mon Son, let's grab some Portillo's and let's go home." As we rode to Portillo's, I kept a force field around the car until we entered the drive through.

CHAPTER 3 - A HUSBAND'S LOVE

As we drove up to our house in Hyde Park, I saw that the living room lights were on. Of course, with Bradley being our first born, my wife stayed up. I had to prepare Bradley for what was to come.

"Bradley, now when we get in here, yo mama gon' ask you what happened. Let me tell her. It will make it easier if I tell her." I told her.

"What about Alicia, Pops?" Bradley asked.

"Oh yeah, you know what to do. Don't let her touch you."

"Got it."

"Now, yo mama is intuitive, so she's going to know that something happened. Just tell her that you're tired and you want to go to sleep. Knowing her, she may have already called Saffore to see what happened."

"Okay," he said as we fist bumped. "Thanks, Pops."

"For what, Son?"

"For taking care of us. We wouldn't be able to get through without you."

"It's my job, Son."

We walked into the house. My wife was standing there washing dishes and listening to her audiobooks.

"We're back, Viv," I said so she could look up.

"I know, I felt you all pull up. So what happened?"

"Nothing much, Mama. Can we talk about it tomorrow? I'm kind of tired," my son said as he walked up to his mother and kissed her on the cheek.

"You sure, baby?" she asked as she hugged him for a long time. I'm sure she wished she had Alicia's gift at this point. Even though she didn't have Ali's gift, she could still tell something was up.

"Yeah Ma, I just need some sleep. Imma take a shower and get some rest." Bradley responded.

"Okay baby, go ahead. Did you eat?" My wife asked.

"Yeah, Pops bought us some Portillo's."

"Okay baby, I love you."

"I love you too, Ma." My son walked upstairs. What did I tell you? Right hand man. He was half way to his room when my wife started giving me the third degree. It's funny, I was a lawyer, but at home, my wife did all the questioning.

"So it's that bad that you told him not to tell me?" she started.

"Viv, I knew you would be upset if he talked about it, so I felt it would be better if you heard it from me. I'm tired too, let's head upstairs and we can talk about it in our room?" I said.

"Sylvester, what's wrong with him? Just tell me."

"Let me shower first."

While I was taking my shower and my wife was in bed waiting for the story, I knew this wasn't going to be easy. When I was done, she was in bed, arms folded. It was time.

"So Bradley can shoot bullets." I came right out and said it.

"So he's bullet proof *and* he's a weapon?" She looked worried.

"Yes, but that's not all." She just stared at me. "Once he shoots the bullets out, they are reabsorbed into his body. So it's like they go out of him, and like a magnet they are attracted back to him."

"Oh Lord."

"That's not all."

"More?"

"It happens when he's really scared or really angry, and when it happens, his skin disappears, and all you see is his steel skeleton. And his biggest fear is not protecting us.

Mainly something happening to me and you all having to depend on him to protect the family."

"Why would he feel like that? How did you know that was his worst fear?"

"Saffore connected him to some virtual reality machine. He had a meter from one to ten. As he turned the meter up, Bradley's fears intensified. And that was his worst fear. He said I had died, and he had to protect you all. Viv, he's scared and wants to learn to control it."

"He's scared? I'm scared."

"Viv, please?"

"No, Sylvester, my baby is bulletproof. Yes, great, every Black mama's dream. I don't have to worry about him being hurt or killed, but he's also a weapon. Do you realize how people would want to weaponize him if they find this out?"

"I do. Saffore and I talked about that."

"His body changes when he's scared," she said, and I could tell she was scared.

"I know, but his body changing is just a part of puberty."

"Sylvester, this isn't puberty, this is his life. I don't think we should do this mission. It's the split that's causing him to be in fear, isn't it?"

"Yes, Viv, but I promise that I won't let anything happen to you all. And he'll be with you. You won't let anything happen to him either." My wife began to cry. She hadn't cried like this since we found out she had super powers. Usually my wife doesn't cry. A Black woman's tears aren't received well. It's because of the toxic view that they're supposed to be strong. For some, crying is a sign of weakness, or they may not get the response of comfort and help that they need. Other times they have to be strong for everyone around them, so they don't get a chance to cry. But in this moment, she needed to let go, and she knew I was here to be strong for her. To be her support, her comfort, her help. To be her man.

"He's already been through enough, I just don't want him to feel like there is something wrong with him," she said between the tears.

"I know, I don't want him to feel that way either, but I want him to learn to control this. He's like this, and we can't change it. So all we can do is help him. God made him like this Viv, and God doesn't make mistakes." I assured her as I hugged her.

Knock. Knock. Knock.

"Mommy, Daddy, can I sleep with you?" It was our baby girl Allena. At the sound of Allena's voice, my wife got out of bed, went into our bathroom and closed the door so she could wipe her tears. She would never let her kids see her cry.

"Sure baby, come in," I said. Lena walked in as cute as can be and wanted me to pick her up.

"Daddy, what happened with you and Bradley?" Allena asked.

"Oh, nothing, baby we just had to see Uncle Saffore, that's all," I said.

"Where's Mama?"

"I'm in here, baby, I just needed to use the bathroom. I'll be out in a sec." See what I mean? No tears. My wife walked out as if she hadn't been crying and sat in bed with me and Lena.

"Daddy, what did Uncle Saffore say? Where is Bradley?" Allena asked.

"He's asleep, baby, just like you should be." I responded.

"No he's not, he was just in the hallway trying to get away from Alicia. She's trying to get him to tell her what happened." Just then, Bradley opened the door to our room and came by our bed.

"Pops, you gotta help me. Alicia is trying to hug me so I have to tell her what happened," Bradley said.

"Boy, I told you to never just come into me and your mama's room. You knock first," I said.

"I know, Pops, but you told me not to let her touch me, and she won't stop chasing me," Bradley said frantically.

"Daddy, why don't you want Alicia to tell him what happened?" Allena asked me. Just then, Alicia popped into our room.

"Daddy, why doesn't Bradley want to tell me what happened?" Alicia asked.

"Wait, girl, stop right there. Stop chasing your brother around," my wife demanded. "And don't walk into our room asking my husband questions like you grown and you his mama."

"I'm sorry, Ma, I just want to know what happened," Alicia walked towards our bed and sat on the end of it while Bradley stood next to me so Alicia won't come by him.

"Why is everyone in here?" Wilson and Calhoun walked up now.

"It looks like this where the party at, Wil, and they didn't tell us. It ain't a party 'til we get here," Cal said.

"Twins, there is no party, we're just trying to figure out what happened with Bradley tonight," Alicia said.

"Oooooh, bro so what happened?" Wilson asked.

Bradley just looked at me.

"Alright, twins, come in and sit down with everyone else," I told them. "So Bradley can shoot bullets." I just came out and said it again.

"Dang," Calhoun and Wilson said at the same time as they sat on the couch in our room.

"Pay up, twins," Allena said, holding her hand out towards them and wiggling her fingers.

"What is this?" my wife asked.

"Us girls bet the boys that Bradley could shoot bullets," Alicia explained

"Don't be placing bets on my son," my wife said.

“Right, y'all betting on me. Being able to shoot from my body is something big to find out. I actually went through a lot today,” Bradley said.

“I’m sorry bro, but a bet is a bet. It’s just candy,” Alicia said.

“That’s not all. He doesn’t just shoot the bullets,” I continued.

“Well what else does he do, Daddy?” Allena asked me as I was still holding her.

“Well, baby, he can reabsorb the bullets. You see, they come back to him like a magnet.”

“I can also expose my steel skeleton. And it happens when I get really scared and really angry,” Bradley explained.

“Bro, that’s deep,” Wilson said.

“And did y'all know that Saffore drank the elixir as well, and that's why he’s so smart?” I asked, trying to lighten the mood.

"What?" everyone said at the same time.

"Daddy, don't change the subject. Now B, how did you find out you could do this and when it happens?" Alicia said.

"Saffore gave me, like, this virtual reality helmet, and it had a meter from one to ten. When it got up to ten all of my worst fears seemed to pop up, and I started reacting. It's like I went blank," Bradley explained to the group.

"Oh, like you asking Uzuri out and her saying no?" Ali asked. So that's who his crush was.

"Ali, I told you that in confidence," Bradley said with eyes big.

"Never mind that, what's your worst fear?" Allena asked. Bradley just got quiet.

"Protecting us all, protecting your dad, and not being able to save us," my wife spoke up, and everyone was quiet.

"I know that doing this helped me to understand my powers more, and it will help me to become a better superhero, but it was hard to come to this," Bradley said.

"I'm glad I did it, and I'm glad I found this out, but it was hard to do to become better."

"Becoming better in any way is hard. When you had to become better at baseball, you had to practice and put your body through pain. It's the same thing," I assured Bradley.

"B, why you worried about protecting us though? We protect each other," Calhoun said, but I could tell he was trying to lighten the mood, like me. He gets his funny spirit from me. "Like I don't need you to protect me because you're older, I'm already stronger."

"Wooow," Bradley said. At least a smile was on his face but I could tell he was a bit taken aback at what Cal had said.

"And I'm smarter and faster," Allena said.

"And I can heal myself and everyone else," Wilson said.

"And I know what everyone is feeling. And to stay home and hide in my room and write if things get too crazy or if everyone isn't feeling good," Alicia said, we all started to laugh.

"I'm glad y'all don't need me," Bradley said.

"Naw, B, we do, but we need each other. We protect each other. So whenever you feel that you can't stand, we're right here to stand with you," Wilson said. Bradley looked happy. I don't know why I was trying to keep all of this from them. Wil was right. We did need each other, and without each other, nothing worked. That was what being a family was. We held each other up.

"Thanks, Wil," Bradley said.

"Daddy, do the rest of us have gifts we don't know about? Or can our gifts get stronger from this machine?" Alicia asked.

"Yeah, I want to find out what else I can do too," Calhoun asked.

"No. Not right now. We'll talk about this another day. It's time for bed," my wife interjected.

“But Ma, why does Bradley get to go and we don’t? We want to know what we can do too,” Calhoun asked, and all my kids gave my wife that puppy dog look.

“Because I said so,” my wife fired back. “And I said it was time for bed. So maybe all of you will be able to find out what you can do. But not today.”

“Yes, Mama, but can I sleep in here tonight?” Allena asked. “You sent us to bed early, and I want to watch a movie.”

“Yeah, I’m not sleepy either after finding this out,” Alicia said.

“Okay you all can stay in here, and we can watch a movie,” I said. Thank God we bought a California king size bed. That night, my kids ended up falling asleep in our room. I could tell my wife was still upset and scared. She just kind of watched Bradley all night. He slept on the couch in our room. The twins slept in their sleeping bags on the floor. Allena slept at the top with us, and Alicia slept at the foot of the bed. My wife put a blanket over all of our kids. When she got to Bradley and placed the blanket over him, she stood there as he slept. I went up to her and hugged her from behind.

“Don’t worry, I promise you I will never let anything happen to him or any of them,” I told her.

CHAPTER 4 - PROTECTOR AND PRIEST

Today was the day that my family and I sat down with the police chief to discuss the plan and what we're tackling. We were unsure if there would be a hate monster again like the one we fought together for Bradley. Or if this would be a person that we would have to take down. With the news about Bradley still lingering in everyone's mind, we decided as a family that it wouldn't be wise to split up. Well, my wife decided. In order for us to do this mission, we had to stick together. We were at the chief's office telling him the plan.

"So Sly, Splendid Saba, what is the plan?" The chief asked.

"Chief, we decided splitting up our family is not the best way to complete this mission. Our kids are still strengthening their gifts and still need guidance. So all the kids will go with Sylvester into Englewood and find out where all of the guns are coming from and what's going on. I will come to the Chicago Public Safety Headquarters and learn their system to find out what's going on in the CPD," my wife explained. I wondered how the kids and I will be with my wife gone.

"So at what point will you join them? Or they will join you?" the chief asked.

"We're not sure. However long it takes for us to find out the information we need," I explained to the chief.

"Okay, that sounds good. So where will you all stay?" the chief asked.

"I'll stay in a hotel, and Sylvester and the kids will stay in the apartment building of an old friend," I responded.

"Great! We can pay for the hotel expenses.," the chief stated. "Now, how do you plan about doing this? Will you all stay in your superhero form or come in your human form?"

"The kids and Sylvester will be in superhero form while they're in Englewood asking questions," my wife responded. "They know a few people who are willing to talk. This will be mostly at night. During the day, he may have to work, and the kids will strengthen their gifts with Saff while he's at work. When I come to the Headquarters, I'll be out of superhero form so I can get as much information as possible. We'll communicate through these devices that Saffore created for us."

"Perfect!" the chief said, excitedly. "While there, make sure you don't say anything about this mission. We'll pretend that you're a new employee there. We'll put you undercover and get you a new I.D. and everything. No one knows your identity in the department, not even the superintendent, so you mustn't tell anyone. Some people may recognize you because of the work you do, but just tell them you get that all the time that you look like yourself, if you know what I mean?" the chief said.

"I can also wear a wig and glasses if that helps?" my wife responded.

"That works for me! Now, you all said there are some people you can ask, do we have any leads so far?" the chief asked.

"I know there are a few people that have informed me that they know where they're getting the guns from, chief. Some people are selling them. That's who we need to tackle first in my old neighborhood. We're hoping from there, it may lead us to some other people," I told the chief.

"In your department, Chief, we're trying to find some connections in the shooting of an unarmed Black teenager that happened a couple months back. I think we'll end up finding that these events aren't disconnected," my wife told the chief. There she was, being intuitive.

"Maybe we'll also find out how the guy who shot at our school also got his gun," Bradley said.

"You all have this all planned out. So when do you want to get started?" the chief asked.

"It's the end of May right now. So once the kids are done with school. We'll focus on this over the summer,." My wife told the chief. "That's why they'll practice their gifts with Saffore during the day."

"Alright, sounds splendid," the chief said with a smile.

We all piled into the car to head home. After talking with the chief, the kids started to ask questions.

"Mama?" Alicia asked.

"Yes, baby?" My wife responded.

"We stopped talking about it last night, but I think it's fair for all of us to find out what we can do. Not just Bradley." Alicia said.

"Y'all didn't even care about y'all gifts until I wanted to know more about mine," Bradley said angrily.

“I know, but we want to know too. And we didn’t know that we could have extra gifts before,” Calhoun said.

“Yeah, like what if we all can do things that we didn’t know about?” Wilson said.

“I thought Alicia called Mama, not y'all,” I said to get the kids quiet. “Well, Viv, what do you think?”

“Well, before we start this mission, I definitely think it is a good idea for our whole family to find out what they can do. This is a big mission, and there is no telling what we’ll find,” my wife said.

“I agree. Should we talk to Saffore?” I asked.

“I definitely think so. Kids, do you understand what this means?” my wife asked. “Just like Bradley was triggered by what he saw, you all could be too. This is very big and it’s important. It can be very traumatic,” my wife informed the kids.

“We understand, Mama, and we’re ready,” Alicia assured her.

“Mama, this will only make us stronger as superheroes. We’ll be okay, and this will help us to help other people,” Calhoun said.

“Okay, I think this will be good for us,” my wife said.

“I’m going to miss you while we’re away from you, Mama,” Lena told my wife. The rest of the kids just looked at my wife. I knew they all would miss her. We’d never done a mission like this and been away from one another.

“It’s alright Lena, I’ll help you with anything you need,” Alicia told her.

“I’m going to miss you too, baby. All of you, but I know you all will help one another,” my wife said.

PART 3: SAMSON AND SICKLE CELL

CHAPTER 1: PHILIPPIANS 4:13

My name is Calhoun, Calhoun, Calhoun Stanton

I'm strong like Samson.

Solid as a rock,

Super long locs,

Popular on TikTok.

Splendid Seven, and I'm Ferocious Number Five

Weak but I thrive

Sickle cell gets me down but I strive

Why must I dive?

Slower and slower into pain
This life is insane,
But you can't see a rainbow without the rain
I try to refrain,

From letting sickness get me down
My twin brother sticks around
Picks me up when my body lets me down
Down, down, I keep falling but not failing
Red blood cells sickle, but I keep prevailing

Battling many wounds
Healing from the one that was with me in the womb

Wil is my healer, my defender, no pretender
Real one 'til the end.

God, why'd you give my family this weight?
Are we really this great?
The city of big shoulders is starting to break.
Can we handle our fate?
Faith, Faith, Faith

I can do all things through Christ who gives me strength
Still don't understand my requirements
Super strong, so I guess that's what He blessed me with.

But then I fall
Too weak to keep up with them all
This Black boy is super strong
But starting to feel real small.

Writing isn't really my thing. Since the school shooting that happened at my big brother and sister's school, Uncle Saff wanted all of us to write down our feelings about being kids and superheroes. He said he wanted us to get how we feel down on paper. That hopefully one day we can share this with our children, and our children's children. TikTok and YouTube are really my thing. But since I can't share my superhero identity and real identity on social media, writing is the only way to do this. I think when I grow up, I'll probably show my true identity to people.

Ali is the writer in our family. I'm more into music. What is a thirteen-year-old boy supposed to talk about exactly? I mean, sometimes I'm confused. I'm the strongest one in my family. Then I'm the weakest and need my twin brother to save me. I'm the loudest and the funniest, and I think that being a superhero is the best thing in the world. My big brother and sister don't agree, but me and Wil know that this superhero thing will always be a part of our lives.

My big brother Bradley has found out about his gifts, but I wish I could know more about mine. Am I stronger than I think? If I push myself too much, will my pain get worse? What if Wil can heal me for good and I don't have to be weak anymore?

"Calhoun! Calhoun! Wake up, Mr. Stanton!" my teacher Ms. Grace called.

"Oh, I'm sorry Ms. Grace," I responded. This class is so boring, but it's the only time I could get writing done. "What were you saying?"

"We only have two weeks left of school, Mr. Stanton. Please pay attention. Tell me the difference between prose and poetry?" Ms. Grace asked again.

If we only had two weeks left, why were we still talking about this stuff? It's not like there would be a test.

"Prose is more like writing a story," I began to respond. "And poetry is like making a song, I guess."

“That’s pretty good, and which do you prefer?” Ms. Grace asked me.

“I guess poetry because it’s like a song.”

“Yeah, my brother loves music. That’s why we’re so popular on TikTok,” Wil said, smiling.

“Alright everyone, class is over. Make sure to write an example of prose or poetry for class next week. Last month, or May, was Asian and Pacific Islander heritage month. April was Arab American heritage month. February was Black History Month. November was Native American heritage month. And September - October was Hispanic heritage month. Whatever you identify as, I want you to come up with some sort of prose or poetry to talk about your heritage. And if you are multiple races, we don’t have a month for that yet, so talk about what that means to you,” Ms. Grace told us.

"Ms. Grace, I'm of multiple races, and I think we should sign a petition for July or August to be multicultural heritage month," Umoja, a girl in my class said.

"I think that's a wonderful idea Umoja, let's do that. Alright everyone, class dismissed." Ms. Grace replied, finally class was over.

"Aye Cal, what were you doing when Mrs. Grace called on you?" Wil asked as we left class and headed towards our lockers.

"Writing down some lyrics," I responded. "I don't like writing, so I decided to put my feelings into music. Since Uncle Saff and Mama want us to write."

"Well don't do it here. Someone might end up seeing what you're writing."

"I don't understand why we have to keep everything a secret. What would really happen if people found out about our family?" I asked.

"The government would probably split up our family and run a bunch of tests on us. And then use us as human weapons. Especially Bradley," Wil said.

"Yeah, you're probably right. How come Bradley gets to learn about all of his gifts and we don't?"

"Well Mama said we'll be going to see Uncle Saffore once school lets out. You ready for track practice?" Wil asked me.

"Yeah." Track wasn't my first choice for a sport, but because of my strength, my mom and dad didn't want me doing any contact sports. I might hurt other team members or opposing team members. I wanted to play football, basketball, or even do boxing, but they said I couldn't. I guess I should be grateful I could play any sport.

"Are you going to art class?" I asked Wil.

"Yeah, I'm thinking instead of writing, I may draw more pictures of how I feel," Wil said.

"Mama might not like that," I told him.

“I don’t know why we have to write anyway. Ali can just write down what we all feel anyway after she holds our hand,” Wil said annoyed.

“Yeah, I guess you’re right.”

“Do you need me to come to track practice with you?” Wil asked me.

“No, I think I should be okay. I’ve never had a sickle cell crisis during practice.”

“Alright, stay hydrated,” Wil told me as he tapped me on the shoulder.

Having sickle cell could be the worst sometimes. It kept me from doing everything. And there were times when I would have a crisis at school and just couldn't participate because I was in so much pain. It usually happened when I was dehydrated. Or when the weather was nice outside and my school had the air conditioner on and I got cold. This was when Wil and I would go into the boy’s bathroom and lock the door, and he’d heal me. Even though I want to play other sports, running was a great way to take my mind off of everything. Running was the closest thing to flying, and it made me feel free. I wondered if that's how Allena felt since she can run faster than the speed of light. There were times when she held my hand and I was able to run fast with her. It feels like you're lost in time, everything around you slowing down. It was great to have everyone slow down but me because sometimes that's what having sickle cell felt like. Everyone was moving fast and I was the only one slowing down.

"So Cal, you'll be leading us today. You'll run the first 400 meters, and then Jamal you'll do the same after Cal passes the baton to you. Both of you are trying to beat your previous running time," my coach told us after we finally were dressed for practice.

I always felt like my cousin Jamal and brother Wil made a deal, and that was why Jamal joined track with me. I felt like Jamal watched out for me since I didn't want Wil to join me in track. Wil wasn't good at running anyway.

"Yes Coach," Jamal and I said at the same time.

Everytime I ran, I always worried about my body failing me. Exercise dehydrates you, and dehydration isn't the best thing for sickle cell.

"Alright Jamal you ready?" Coach asked.

"Ready Coach!" Jamal was at the end of the track.

"Cal, you ready?"

"I stay ready Coach!" The whistle sounded off. Three, two, one, run!

Foot strikes asphalt.
Moving like a thunderbolt.
Beads of sweat taste like salt.

Sweat? Wait!
Gotta make sure I hydrate.

Still running, gotta accelerate.

Feet make a steady cadence.
Sickle cell pain improved my perseverance.
Being superhuman improves my endurance.

Getting a runner's high.
Endorphins got me feelin' like I can fly.
I feel alive.

Moving fast like a jet.
Think I can't win this race?
Aight, bet!
See the look on my face.
No longer in this place.
Flying so high, I'm in outer space.

So this is what it means to be free.

My body isn't stopping me.

Full of energy like it's supposed to be.

Almost to Jamal to pass the baton.

Race already been won.

Almost done.

Start to slow down.

Feet on the ground.

Great job Cal! Hydrate and sit down.

"Great job Cal! Come over and sit down," Coach told me.

"Yes Coach!" I breathed heavily.

"You okay?"

"Yeah Coach, I'm good!" Just gotta get hydrated.

"Great job, Jamal!" The coach said.

The last day of school was finally here. It was a fun day, saying goodbye to all of our friends and playing some summer games at school. Regardless, I was glad summer break was here. I couldn't believe we had one more year, and then Wil and I would be high schoolers. I hadn't had a crisis in over a month, and we got to see Uncle Saff to learn more about our gifts. Then we'd get started with our mission. Life had been so good. I didn't know how to describe how I felt. So I told Ali to give me a word after she held my hand today. She said I was nervous and excited, so anxious. She also saw me not having a crises anymore. She told me that this probably wouldn't happen, but having super strength was already a big accomplishment.

Our parents took us to see Uncle Saff to prepare us for the big mission. We'd be strengthening our gifts all summer with him. They dropped us off at his lab so we could have our time with Uncle Saff without any interruptions from our dad or fear from our mom.

"Alright nieces and nephews, today is the day you find out if your gifts go deeper than you think. Now, I've designed a test for each of you. So based on the gifts you already have, I made some predictions. I won't tell you what they are. I just want to see what happens. After studying Bradley, I realize that his newfound gifts may be from puberty. So Alicia, you may have more gifts. Cal and Wil, you may have more gifts. But little Lena, you may not have newfound gifts yet. Also, we're still trying to strengthen the ones you do have. We definitely need to do this before you all embark on the gang and gun violence mission," Uncle Saff told us while we were in his lab and he set up the room for all of our tests.

"So Uncle Saffore I won't have any new gifts?" Allena asked, disappointed.

"No niecy wiecy, but we will do some practices and strengthen your current gifts," Uncle Saff responded.

"Okay," Allena said sadly.

"Don't be sad, you'll be able to get more gifts one day. Now, all of you may not have new gifts. Wilson, we'll start with you. We all know you can heal and understand and speak many languages. But your healing power is temporary if someone is born with a condition. Like Cal, for example, with his sickle cell. I want to see if you can heal someone who's been sick long term."

When Uncle Saffore said this, I was excited. This is what I'd been hoping for.

"So in the lab, we have organs that people are donating. People who are deceased, of course. I want to see if you're able to bring life back into the organs or if you can reverse the organs back to health. This may take some time, and just like Bradley, your gifts may improve if you're under pressure. So your virtual reality will be inside a hospital, and your patient, who's a smoker, will be going into cardiac arrest. Now, I know you can stop the heart attack if the person is alive, but I will intensify the virtual reality to see if you are able to bring their heart back to life and if you're able to reverse their lungs back to health. The virtual reality is timed, so every three minutes it will intensify."

"Sounds good, Unc," Wil said.

"Good! Now Ali, you can feel other people's feelings and see their memories. But you can't read minds, and that may change once we do this test. Now, I know you don't want to read people's minds since feeling their pain is enough. Learning to let go of their pain and horrible memories is your challenge. As you all embark on this mission you may feel more pain and see more horrible memories than you have before. You may not be able to block those things out, and we want to avoid you holding on to these things and it affecting you. We want to avoid this happening. You're going to hold Bradley's hand, and as your virtual reality intensifies, he will let your hand go and we will see if you can read his mind."

"Got it!" Alicia said. Now it was my turn.

"Next, Cal, we want to see if there is a way for you to be able to use your super strength even if you're having a sickle cell crisis. So I'm going to inflict pain on you with this machine. It will feel a lot like sickle cell pain. The pain will intensify as I turn the meter up, but I still want you to try to lift this 1,000-pound weight."

"Got it." I was scared about the physical pain I would feel, but I wanted to know if I could still use my power even while having a crisis. I knew that no matter what, this would only make me stronger, if that was possible. Uncle Saff started all of us off using our tests. What's crazy though, we all had to do the tests at the same time. He intensified all of our realities at the same time using his tablet. I don't know how my uncle did it, but all of our virtual realities saw something different, but everything was synced to his tablet. The weight was getting hard for me to lift when Saff turned the meter up to six, but I was able to block out the pain and keep lifting. By this time, Bradley had moved his hand from

Ali and Wil was trying to reverse the lungs back to normal. When he turned the meter up to eight I was about to drop the weight, my legs started to give out. What I could hold with one hand between zero and five on the meter, I was now holding with two hands. The meter was now on ten. My arms were about to give out, and the weight was about to fall. I closed my eyes, and all of our realities were at ten on the meter. I screamed so loud and so hard from trying to keep the weight up through the pain. When I opened my eyes, I was still holding the weight. Wilson's hand was on my leg, giving me strength and stopping the pain. Ali had run over to me. How did she know where I was standing if she still had the virtual reality helmet on? Uncle Saff had finally cut the machine off. I didn't feel the pain anymore, and Ali and Wil's virtual realities had gone blank.

"Splendid," Uncle Saff said as he stopped the machine.

CHAPTER 2: GALATIANS 6:2

"So Saff, what happened today?" My dad asked when he and my mom returned.

"The kids did splendidly. I gave each of them a test, but I gave it to them simultaneously. So when the meter reached eight, Bradley moved his hand, and Alicia couldn't read his mind. But Bradley also wasn't in pain. I wanted to distract Alicia with Bradley to see if she would stay focused on him instead of Calhoun. I had the kids place their virtual reality helmets on before I started the test. Alicia didn't know exactly where I placed Calhoun in the room, but was able to come to him because she sensed his pain. It's like even under the pressure of virtual reality and holding Bradley's hand, she could still sense Cal's pain. Sensing his pain helped her to know where he was. Her heightened senses helped her to track his hurt and come to him. Even without being able to see. She also wasn't distracted by the virtual reality, which was saving Bradley."

"So do you think she can do this with anyone, Saff?" My dad asked.

"Maybe, depending on their proximity to her. I'll have to run some more tests. But she doesn't just have to hold someone's hand to feel pain. Her sense of pain is heightened when another person's pain is heightened."

"But Uncle Saff, I can't help anyone once I feel their pain? So what's the point?" Ali asked.

"The point is, Ali, you can lead others to the person in intense pain just by feeling it. Imagine if you all are on a mission and someone is hurt. You can lead an ambulance, firefighters, or even Wilson to them to help them to heal them. The breathe and block techniques also worked because you didn't let what was going on with Bradley and feeling what he felt, distract you from helping someone else. You knew how to block out his feelings to be able to help Cal. As for Wilson, you weren't able to make the dead heart start beating again. So you can't revive something that has died. But at about notch 9, you were able to reverse the lung damage. So if an illness is not a congenital disorder like Calhoun's sickle cell, a person can still be healed forever. You were able to reverse the lung damage for good, unlike the congenital disorders. So diseases, illnesses, or disorders that people aren't born with can be reversed by your power and healed for good. What I noticed when it came to Calhoun is that you were able to lessen his pain as you have done before. But because of you hearing his screams you came to him to heal him. Of course, you removed the helmet, which you weren't supposed to do, but you felt that your brother needed you."

"But Unc, that's nothing new," Wil said.

"I know, but this has to do with your twin connection. You knowing that he needs healing heightened your need to come to him and help him. I did this on purpose. I distracted you to see if you would still be able to come to Cal to help him when he called out to you. It's like it was instinctual. I also wanted you all to see that it's not just about finding new gifts like Bradley has, which is great. Or strengthening your gifts like Lena, which is important. It's about you all working together to strengthen each other. Once I told Bradley to let go of Alicia's hand, I told him to leave the room and stand outside. I knew that once everyone saw Calhoun struggling, they would come to him. The Bible says that you all are supposed to strengthen each other, and that's what this test was all about. When you heard Calhoun scream or felt his anguish, would you help him? That is what I wanted to find. You all passed!"

"What about me, Unc?" I asked. I wanted to know since he was congratulating Wil and Ali.

"What I noticed about your test is that you were able to still lift that much weight even in pain. You used your brain to enhance your brawn. Before Ali and Wil made it over to help you, you were able to keep lifting the weight even when your pain was intensified. Wil healed your limbs after I turned off the pain inflictor even though you weren't having a crisis. So there wasn't anything really to heal, but you kept being strong regardless of the pain. Your sickle cell may cause you bodily harm, but it doesn't stop your super strength mentally and physically. Now your strength did diminish as the pain intensified. This could mean that if you were to have a crisis in the middle of a mission, you may not be as strong as you usually are."

Uncle Saff was really impressed with our abilities. Even though it seemed as if we hadn't learned a lot about ourselves, we learned what we needed to know. That we need each other. We all had our gifts because we could use them to not only help Chicago, but to strengthen each other.

Uncle Saff told us to come back again before we started the mission in a couple of weeks for more tests, before we started strength training for our gifts. Wil may not have been able to heal my sickle cell, but it was good to know that he could heal my pain. It was good to know that Ali could feel my pain. Regardless of my pain, I could still use my power.

My dad took the family out to dinner at Giordano's to celebrate how well we did.

"So how you feelin', ferocious number five?" My dad asked me as my mom hugged me while we were eating dinner.

"I feel okay. I wish I didn't have sickle cell anymore or didn't have a crises anymore. But it feels good to know that I can still use my power no matter my pain. And that Ali knows how I feel and Wil can heal me for a while. Even if it can only be for that moment in time," I responded.

"I always got you, bro," Wil told me.

"Yeah, and even when you get on my nerves, I got you too. I'm glad that I was able to block out everything that was going on around me when Cal needed me. I couldn't read Bradley's mind, and he wasn't in anguish anyway. But it was like once Cal was hurt and I felt his pain, even from afar, I just automatically came to him." Ali said.

"Well I'm proud of you all for taking all of this in and being okay with it. I didn't originally want us to do this, but I felt that it was necessary before we start our mission in a couple weeks. I also felt that it's important for you to understand your gifts and work together since I'll be separated from you. So I'm glad we did this. I feel more comfortable with leaving knowing that you all will take care of each other," Mama said. "How did you all feel after using the pain inflictor?"

"It hurt, but I was okay," I responded. "I'm glad to find out what I can do today. Like Bradley said, it will only help to make us better heroes."

"Yeah, I didn't see anything too crazy inside my virtual reality. It showed me operating on someone, but I get why we need to do this. In order to protect and save others, and complete this mission, this is a step in that direction," Wilson said.

"Yeah, I agree," Ali said. "Well thank God we didn't go with the chief's idea to separate."

"Chief? Sylvester, I thought it was your idea to separate," my mom said to my dad, giving him that look she gave when we were in trouble.

"Mama, I'm sorry, I meant to say Daddy's idea," Ali said. Nice save.

Mind and matter

With both we are better

Better together, brains and brawn

Splendid Seven is the number one

Number one family in the windy city

We take no pity

Gifts not inhibited by proximity

Bearing others' burdens, feeling others' pain

Healing others' wounds just the same

Super strength even in our pain.

Bones made of steel

Bullets coming in and out like a movie reel

Speaking many tongues

My family's so poppin' our song can never be unsung.

Keen intuition, strong premonition

Bringing an end to gun violence to fruition

Running as fast as the speed of light

Hiding our true identities by night

Expansive force fields that surround Illinois

Splendid Saba brings this Black boy joy

Power mimicry, awesome abilities

The best Black superhero family of the 21st century.

After strengthening our gifts with Uncle Saff, it was finally time for us to start with this mission. Before we took on any assignment, my family would always pray. We definitely needed to pray today since this would be the biggest mission we'd ever gone on. Uncle Saff was with us today at the chief's house so he could pray with us before we set off on our mission.

"Father, we come to you today to ask that you bless the Splendid Saba as you already have. Bless them, Lord, to use their abilities to solve the problems that plague Chicago and the rest of America. To find those that are infecting our city with this gang and gun violence. We ask that You strengthen this family to protect one another, to heal one another, to watch over one another, to control their anger, to control their feelings, and stand strong even in their pain. Amen."

It made us a little sad to think that we were going to be separated from Mama, and we didn't know for how long. Two big black trucks with tinted windows pulled up, and all of us piled into one while our mama got in the other. Lena cried after hugging Mama when it was time for us to go. And even though the rest of us didn't cry, we were still upset that she couldn't come. During the ride, Lena was still crying, and Ali was holding her trying to cheer her up. I told her I would get her some candy and we would call Mama once we got back to the apartment.

"And don't worry. I'll be able to get you juice boxes and do your hair," Ali told her. I guess since she was holding her, she knew how she felt. When we arrived at the apartment, it had three bedrooms. One for dad, one for us guys, and one for the girls. I was used to sharing a room with Wil but not B. He was going to be annoyed, I thought.

“Pops, is this your friend's place? It’s so small. Where are we supposed to fit?” Bradley asked.

“Look y’all, this is temporary.,” my dad said. “It’s not our house in Hyde Park where everyone has their own room. Except for the twins, who share a room. We have two bathrooms here, but we have 4 and a half at home. Don’t act so spoiled. We’re just staying here until we can figure some things out in Englewood. And until your mama is done at headquarters. Look, we all wanted to do this mission. We’re fighting for a bigger cause, and we can’t lose sight of that. So you guys have to be patient. This mission is going to cause you to grow up a bit and so is this place. Being a superhero, saving people, saving Chicago, potentially saving the world, is about sacrifices. Us staying here without Mama is a part of that sacrifice to help other people. And y’all talking about a room, think about the sacrifice Jesus had to make for us,” my dad responded.

“Alright Dad, we won’t complain. This mission is big for our family. This place is just going to take some getting used to,” Ali said.

“Thank you, Bay Bay. Now y’all go into your rooms and start getting your stuff together. Ali, can you help Lena for me?” My dad asked.

“Sure, Dad,” Ali responded.

“Daddy, can we call Mommy now?” Lena asked walking up to my dad.

“Baby girl, how about you help Ali get settled, and we’ll call Mommy after dinner. I’m sure Mommy is getting settled too,” my dad responded. B was right, the place was small. But I understood what my dad was saying. If we couldn’t handle living in this little place, how would we ever handle doing what we had to do to save everyone? I wonder what my mom was doing and if she was missing us.

Ring. Ring. Ring.

"Hello! Hey baby! I'm glad you called, the kids miss you!" my dad said as he answered the phone.

"Mommy! Can I talk to her?" Lena said.

"Lena wants to talk to you, baby, hold on!" My dad told my mom

"Hi Mommy, I miss you! What are you doing?" Lena asked my mom as she held my dad's phone.

"Lena, once you're done let me talk to Mama. I have to ask her where she packed your stuff," Ali said.

"Okay! No, Mommy, we're fine…" Lena continued to talk to our mama.

"Lena, let me talk to Mama, I have to ask her where she packed my art supplies," Wil said.

"WILSON, I JUST GOT ON THE PHONE WITH MOMMY. WAIT," Lena yelled.

"But I got a question to ask her," Wil said as he tried to reach for the phone, but Lena moved away.

“Alright, let me turn on the video chat,” my dad said as he grabbed the phone from Lena. “Alright, it’s up now, she can see everyone.”

“Mama, where did you pack Lena’s stuff for her hair?” Ali asked

“It’s in the small blue bag with Wilson’s art supplies,” my mom responded.

“Thanks Mama!” Wilson said.

“Ma, this place is small, do you see it? How long do you think it’ll take you to figure things out at headquarters?” Bradley asked.

“Mommy, who is going to do my hair, and who is going to cook for us?” Lena asked.

“Alright, everyone calm down. Now yes, the place is small but we want to stay hidden, so we don’t need a big place. No one has lived there for a while, and it’s furnished so it looks good for us to be there right now. Baby girl, Daddy is going to cook for you, and Ali is going to do your hair. I don't know how long it will take me to complete the job at headquarters, but I'll work as fast as I can," my mom assured everyone.

"Baby, you take your time, we'll be okay! Saff and I will hold it down while you get everything under control at headquarters," my dad comforted my mom.

"Cal, you've been quiet, are you okay?" my mom asked me. Sometimes my siblings can be so needy that I fall back. And I usually get so much attention from everyone because of my illness, so I didn't want to hog all of the attention. My mama, being intuitive though, knew that I wanted to talk to her but was trying to stay quiet.

"Yeah Ma, I'm okay," I replied.

"Lena, Mommy will call you guys later and talk to you after I get myself settled. Can you give Calhoun the phone?" Everyone was staring at me. I wasn't my mom's favorite, but with me having sickle cell, she felt like she had to pay me more attention. Sometimes, even if something was wrong, I tried not to say anything because I didn't want my brothers and sisters to get jealous. Only Ali knew this though. So when Lena handed me the phone, Ali walked away to keep getting settled.

"Hey Ma," I said, kind of low.

"Hey baby, are you okay?" My mama asked me.

"Yeah Ma, I'm good!" That's all I said, even though I was sad about her not being with us.

"Okay baby, I'll be back with you all soon. And don't worry, everything will be okay!"

"Okay Ma, love you!" I think Ali told her how we all were feeling.

"I love you too, baby. Give your dad the phone back."

"Yeah babe?" my dad answered my mom.

"Sylvester, turn the phone towards the kids for me," my mama said.

"Kids, your mama has something to say, listen up," my dad said.

"Alright guys, I want you to focus on strengthening your gifts. This is a big mission, and you'll need all the strength you can develop. Make sure you're not giving your dad a hard time. Listen to Uncle Saffore and be good! I'll be with you soon, don't worry. Be patient, be strong, help each other, and protect one another. And please try not to argue. I love you all," my mom told us.

"We love you too, Ma!" we all said. After the conversation with Mama, we were all finally in our rooms unpacking. The room we had to share with Bradley was small. It had a twin sized bed for him, and a bunk bed for me and Wil. There was a tall dresser and a closet for all our things. Wil and I took the dresser and Bradley put his things in the closet. It was tight, but it was all we had right now. After we unpacked Wil got out his art supplies and started drawing on the floor. I took out my headphones and started listening to music at the bottom bunk. Bradley walked in and started looking for his weights.

"I'm looking for my weights, y'all seen 'em?" Bradley asked.

"No, we haven't," Wil said.

"Y'all unpacked?" Bradley asked.

"Yeah, I am," Wil said, "Cal, you unpacked? Cal?" Wil was tapping me. I couldn't hear him because I had my headphones in my ears.

"My bad, Wil, what's up?" I said.

"I said, you unpacked?" Wil asked.

"Oh, yeah," I said.

"Cal, you okay?" Bradley asked me. Even though Bradley was our big brother, we didn't talk to him much. He would always be gone with Ahava, before he passed, or some of his other friends. It was weird to have to share a room with him and talk to him.

"Yeah B, I'm good," I said.

"Aight. I know this room is small, but if we stay out of each other's way we should be fine," Bradley said as he walked out of the room. Typical Bradley, not thinking about us.

"Typical," I said to Wil.

"What? He's going through a lot, Cal," Wil said.

"He's not the only one, Wil, we all are."

"I know, sorry," Wil said. Bradley walked back in with his weights. He sat on his bed and started lifting. Right behind him, my dad came in.

"Hey boys, we'll be going out tonight to ask some of our leads some questions. But we need some milk, and I forgot to grab some. There is a store up the street, can y'all go get some?" My dad asked as he stood in the doorway of our room.

"All of us Pops? Why don't you just want me to go?" Bradley asked, still lifting.

"Cuz, this place is small, and I think you all need some breathing room. Go out, stretch your legs a bit, and grab some milk. Besides, this is my old neck of the woods, and y'all don't know much about it. When you go out, you need somebody else with you to watch yo back. This ain't our place in Hyde Park. Take your little brothers with you and come straight back. Here are the keys to the truck," my dad said as he threw Bradley the keys.

"Aight, Pops," Bradley said. Bradley, Wil, and I drove to the strip mall and parked in the lot next to the store. It was a quiet car drive besides the music playing in the background. Wil looked up to Bradley, so he rode shotgun and tried to talk to him a few times. Bradley only responded with one word answers. Ever since Bradley got to high school we didn't talk to him much. I sat in the backseat with my headphones still in and didn't even try to talk to my big brother. We finally pulled up to the little strip mall with the store that Dad was talking about.

"Y'all want to stay in the car while I get the milk?" Bradley asked us.

"Yeah B, we'll stay in," Wil said.

“Okay, I’ll take the keys with me. Make sure nobody drives off with y’all,” Bradley said.

“Cal, you okay with the air? Are you in pain?” Wil asked me.

“Naw bro, I’m good right now,” I said. When Bradley walked into the store, Wil wanted to get out of the car. He stepped out and saw something he wanted to sketch, so I followed him and stood next to him while he sketched. We locked the doors before we got out. We figured Bradley would be out soon, and then we’d hop back in.

CHAPTER 3: HEBREWS 13:1

While Bradley was in the store and we were in the parking lot of the strip mall, Wil heard a noise. I still had my headphones in.

"Cal?" he said as he was tapping me. "Cal, what is that noise?" I heard ten popping sounds, and some screaming, and then I saw some people running out of another store in the strip mall.

"Aye bro those are gunshots, duck down." We ducked down behind a cooler next to the store, and we saw people running out of the store. Some guys came out while people were still running. While we were down, Wil said that we should run back to the car since it was bulletproof. So we did and tried to open the door, but we forgot we'd locked it.

"Dang, Cal, it's locked. What are we going to do?" Just as Will said that, the police pulled up. Many of them were trying to calm the people down and get inside the store. Where was Bradley? Then one of the cops called to us. I guess two 13-year-old Black boys trying to open the door of black truck with tinted windows looked sus.

"Hey, what are you two doing?" More gunshots went off and people were running, so we decided to run and find somewhere to duck and cover besides the car.

"HEY, STOP!" the cop yelled to us. We started running, and he and another cop ran after us as well. Didn't someone just shoot inside a store? Did he think that it was us? Why was he following us? We kept running, and they kept chasing. Wil wasn't much of a runner and started slowing down. Wil got on my back and wrapped his arms around my neck and I kept running. As I was running, I slipped and fell.

I was so scared that I was looking behind me and not paying attention to where I was going. Rule number one of running track. I know — stupid, right? That I wasn't looking ahead. The cops were behind me and Wil. Guns drawn, staring us down.

"I SAID STOP!" I heard one say.

"That's them, they fit the description," I heard the other say.

Wil and I started to get up to run again.

"FREEZE," they said. I don't remember what happened next; all I remember is hearing the sound of five gun shots and not feeling any pain. When I opened my eyes, my brother Bradley was hovering over Wil and I, absorbing all five bullets. His back was to the police, as was ours. He had us in his arms.

"Don't worry little brothers, I got y'all. Y'all okay?" Bradley had his hoodie on so the cops didn't see his face.

"What's going on?" the cops said; they saw they had shot Bradley, but there was no blood. They shot at him a few more times. He was still hovering over us. Just then, a forcefield appeared around us.

"STOP!" I heard a loud, booming voice say.

"Don't shoot, that's one of our city's heroes," I heard one cop tell the other.

"BOYS, GET UP! GO!" My dad was running up to us and my brothers, and I started running while inside the forcefield. My dad was in his superhero clothes. As we started to run, the cop started to shoot the forcefield, and then he shot at my dad. My dad used Bradley's gifts and made himself bulletproof, so the bullets just bounced right off of him. But it made him angry that the cop tried to shoot him.

"These were suspects in the shooting. This doesn't concern you, we got this," the cop said as my dad got close to them after shooting at him a couple times. My dad stopped and said, "I don't think your chief, CPD, or the world will be thrilled to hear that you all shot at unarmed, innocent, Black children. Did you look at the camera footage? Do you know who the shooters were?" The cops just looked at him.

"Exactly. Let this go. It doesn't have to get out. And if you won't say anything, I won't say anything." The cops looked upset but didn't shoot anymore. We had all ran back to the strip mall parking lot. People were still standing around to tell the cops what happened. People were crying, and we overheard someone say seven people were shot, and one was a child. Only six years old. CBS news was also there.

"You boys okay?" my dad asked us once he got back to the strip mall and talked to us behind the stores.

"Yeah Pops, we're fine," Bradley said. Wil and I were still shaking.

"Let me change back into my regular clothes." Uncle Saff had created bracelets for my family so that when we tapped them, our superhero clothes would come on. When we tapped them again, it would go back to our regular clothes. We hadn't used them yet, but my dad had. It was kind of cool to see it in action even though I was still shaken up.

"Bradley, give me the keys so we can get in the car. Where is the milk?" My dad asked.

"It's by the car, Pops. I noticed that Wil and Cal were gone, so I dropped it and ran to get them." We went back over to the truck, and sure enough, the milk was there. Our car was fine too.

"Sir, is this your car?" A cop asked my dad.

"Yes," my dad responded.

"Did you and your family see what happened?" The cop asked.

"No, we heard the shots, so we ducked down, and we ran when we saw everyone running. Did you all catch who did it?"

"We will, sir."

"If you'll excuse me officer, I'm going to take my boys home where it's safe." We got in the car to drive back home.

"So Bradley, what happened?" my dad asked my big brother while we were driving back to the apartment.

"I went inside to get the milk, Pops. I took the keys with me. Wil and Cal wanted to stay in the car. I don't know what happened after that. I heard the gunshots after I paid for the milk. I ducked and then ran outside to the car. Once I got there, I saw that Wil and Cal were gone. I looked and saw two cops running after them to the left of me. So I started running as I put my hoodie on, and then I called you with the device that Uncle Saff gave us. I got to them before the cops shot at them. Pops, they were down on the ground, unarmed. I don't even know why they would shoot at them?"

"He said we fit the description of the shooters," Wil said.

"Never mind that. Why were you guys out of the car when Bradley went into the store?" my dad said in anger.

“I saw something I wanted to sketch so we stepped out. We knew Bradley had the key, and we didn’t want anyone to get in, so we locked the doors,” Wil said.

“Boys, next time you can’t just get out of the car. If Bradley, me, or Mom goes into the store, you have to stay put. And next time I send you all to the store, you go in with Bradley,” my dad said. I could tell he was frustrated.

“We’re sorry Dad.” I said.

“It’s not your fault, and I’m sorry for being upset. But imagine if Bradley hadn’t made it to you in time. Or if I hadn’t come. Look, Ali and Lena will probably ask what happened. Just tell them you guys forgot to get some money for the milk, so I had to bring you some. If your mother found out, she’d be furious and want to stop everything. Bradley and I do this all of the time. We gotta keep stuff from the girls because it may be too much for them. Are you two sure you’re okay?” My dad asked.

“We’re fine, Dad,” I said.

"Bradley, great job protecting your little brothers, man." My dad said to Bradley.

"No problem, Pops." Bradley responded.

"It's not the same as where we live. You all have to stick together and pay attention. It's not easy being a young Black boy on the streets of Chicago. If the cops don't get you, the gangsters will. You have to be careful. It's my fault. I should've just gone with you."

We were all quiet when my dad said that on our way back to the apartment. When we got there, Ali and Lena asked us what happened, and we told them what Dad had told us to say. Mama called back later on that night. Wil and I pretended to be asleep so Mama couldn't tell that we were shaken up. She did ask why we were asleep so early and knew my dad must have been hiding something. But since she wasn't close to him, she couldn't get him to tell the truth. She thought maybe he had cooked something and it gave us food poisoning.

My dad decided we would go talk to the leads tomorrow. Ali and Lena wanted to know why. He told them that it would be better if we all got some rest. My dad called the chief, and using Lena's eidetic memory, he gave the chief a description of the two cops and told him their names. The chief looked into the issue and the cops were demoted the next day. My dad knocked on our door, came into our room, and then closed it behind him. Then he put a forcefield around us so Ali and Lena couldn't hear us if they were ear hustling.

"Boys, how you feelin'?" My dad asked us as he sat on Bradley's bed. Wil and I were in the bunk bed. Me at the bottom and him at the top. B was sitting in his bed when my dad walked in.

"I don't know Dad, confused. How did the cop say they had a description when the shooters had just shot inside the store and so many people were running out? Was it because we were trying to get in the car? I mean, we're just kids," Wil said.

"Yeah, Wil, y'all are kids but people your age commit crimes all the time. Ahava was your age when we first met him," Bradley said.

"And I see this in court all of the time, boys. Black boys and girls, but especially boys, don't have the luxury of being looked at like kids. When that cop shot at you all, he didn't see kids. When he said you fit the description, it's because you were Black males. Yes you are young, yes you are boys, yes you didn't commit the crime, but that doesn't change anything. I know you all are upset and scared, but think about all of the young kids who don't commit crimes. Or even those who do. But they don't have a big brother who is bulletproof and a dad who is a well-known superhero with force fields to save them. I know it's not fair. I'm not saying that it is, but it's the world we live in, and we have to fight to make it better. This is why we do what we do. This is why our ancestors did what they did. You all remember when we fought the racial hatred monster. Hatred runs through so many people for no reason at all. And we're just trying to stop the hate." My dad tried to explain to us.

"Bradley, thanks for saving us," Wil said. I got up and I hugged him after Wil said this. He was shocked, but he hugged me back. I could tell my dad was happy, and Wil was too.

"Of course. I mean y'all may get on my nerves and annoy me sometimes, but y'all are my little brothers. I'm always here to protect you," Bradley said.

"This is why God blessed us with these gifts, so we can help others. Everyone doesn't have someone like us in their families to protect them or save them. That's why we're here to protect others," my dad said.

That night while we were lying in bed, I felt the need to talk to Bradley. My dad was in his room looking over some things and talking to Uncle Saff. Lena and Ali were in their room. Ali was talking to Zoe and Lena was talking to mom until she fell asleep.

"Bradley?" I began.

"Yeah Cal, what's up?"

"How come you don't ever talk to me and Wil anymore or want to do stuff with us?" Wil was in the top bunk drawing, but he looked over at Bradley.

"I talk to y'all, whatchu mean?" Bradley responded annoyed.

"No Bradley, you don't. We used to be close to you, and it's like once you got to high school, you stopped talking to us," I said.

"I didn't know y'all felt like that. I guess it's a part of me getting older. That's what happens. I got grades, baseball, responsibilities — you know, stuff like that. I have my own friends and everything." I guess he could see from the look on our faces that we were sad, so he went on.

"But that's no excuse. Y'all are my brothers. We have a special bond. So no matter what I do, my life is always going to lead back to you all. Ahava was the only friend I had that knew about our family being superheroes. Now he's gone. But we have a bond because you all know my secret too, and you can relate to me. That's the cool thing about our family having super powers. We don't have to keep it a secret from one another. We can relate to each other. I also kind of stopped talking to you guys a lot because you both are close. You know, it's like you don't need me because y'all got each other."

"What do you mean, B? We want to be close to you," Wil stopped drawing.

"I know, but y'all are twins. Cal, you're super strong. See, you picked Wil up today, put him on your back, and ran with him to save him. And Wil, whenever Cal is having trouble with his sickle cell, you're always there to watch out for him. So you all got each other. And I guess that's why I was close to Ahava, because he knew my secret and was my best friend who had my back. Like you all are best friends and have each other's back. But like you all save and help each other, I wasn't able to do that for him. I didn't have his back like I was supposed to do. The least I could've done for him, was protect him from bullets and I didn't."

"We understand that Bradley, and we're sorry. But we need you too. We're not bulletproof. Where would we be today without you?" Wil told Bradley.

"I guess you're right. I didn't think about that. Look, I didn't mean to be distant, but it's like sometimes I feel I need my own friend who gets me because y'all got that. But I didn't realize that I can have that with y'all. Y'all are my friends who know what I'm going through, and I know what you're going through," Bradley responded.

"We love you too, B." There was Wil again, being the soft one.

"Thanks, Wil. Even though we can relate and I'm your big brother, y'all still annoy me. And I can't wait to have my own room back," Bradley smiled at us. "Now get some sleep, y'all. We got a big night tomorrow."

Megalo adelfos phileo

Tria adelfos phileo

My big brother's love

These three brothers' love

Sharing abilities given from the one above.

Knowing each other's true identity

Fighting for each other with all intensity

Serenity, when ya boy got ya back

Quick with a comeback

Protecting you from any attack

Fixing you when you crack

Carrying you when you lack

Let me fall back

Back to what these two mean to me

Left and right they cover me

In my weakness they comfort me

Me, I don't deserve the brothers I have

When I'm down they make me laugh

It's like Aaron and Hur helping Moses with his staff

Yeah, it's like that

That's what brotherly love means

Sharing the same genes

Responding to each other's needs

Happy with each other's dreams

No jealousy!

No Cain and Abel, no Joseph and the eleven

Fighting side by side because we are the Splendid Seven

Thank you for all you have given

Given to me

Loving me

Healing me

Protecting me

Happily, we'll always be

The Stanton bros. Three.

PART 4: HEALING WOUNDS

CHAPTER 1 - BROTHERLY HATRED

"Wil, you're a fantastic artist!" Ali said standing in the doorway of her and Lena's bedroom at our temporary apartment as I showed her my drawings. "I know Mama and Uncle Saffore want us to write, but I love the way you tell a story with art."

"Thanks, Ali. I wish I could draw what I feel instead of writing. Or you could write it for me?" I tried to low-key ask my sister.

"Nice try, but you're supposed to be writing down your own thoughts and feelings. Here is what you can do. Draw what you feel first, then write it down. Like a description or something."

"That's actually a good idea, I think I'll try it."

"Alright kids, get ready," my dad said. "This will be our first mission tonight, and I don't know where it will lead us, so get ready to suit up in an hour."

"Got it, Dad!" Ali said. "Better get ready," she told me.

As a superhero, I was still having trouble understanding why I had my gifts. So I could heal others, but that didn't seem like a big deal. I wasn't strong like my twin or invincible like my big brother. I wasn't the best fighter or the best runner. So I could just heal people. I mean, I was happy about this ability, but it seemed that it mainly helped my brother with his sickle cell. Then, I could also speak every language. Everyone thought it was so cool. When I thought about it, it was cool when someone was talking in their native tongue and I could respond. But isn't a superhero supposed to be strong and forceful?

I'd thought so much about being a superhero forever. I told Cal that I would be a superhero with him forever, but with my gifts, I felt like this wasn't my thing. I'd thought about it, and maybe I wanted to be a doctor like my Uncle Saff. I mean, I could heal people permanently and temporarily, and I could speak to everyone. I would be a great doctor. Ever since the pandemic came and brought to light the injustices that Black people face within the medical field, I thought having a Black male doctor who could speak different languages and heal people would help tremendously. It sucked to think that Black mothers have the highest infant mortality rate. Or that people believe, and have believed, that Black people don't feel pain. I knew that my twin definitely felt pain, and lots of it. I wished I could help more people like I helped Cal.

We were getting ready for our first night out talking to people in Englewood. Hopefully they'd inform my dad of where the guns were coming from and maybe make some connections to the CPD. I was still trying to understand how I fit into all of this. Why were my gifts important? What did I bring to the table as a superhero? We were all in a black truck with tinted windows given to us by the chief. But when we're out at night, my dad put a forcefield around it so no one could see us. That way, when we drive in the morning, no one would make any connections to our family.

"Alright kids," my dad began to explain this mission to us. "So we're about to go speak with some of the kids that we caught during the carjacking at the car dealership."

"But Daddy, why would they give us any information? We caught them," Ali asked.

"Because while I was representing them in court, I told them that the superheroes, had told me as their lawyer to get the judge to let them off easy," my dad reassured us.

"They've been doing community service at the community center over here in Englewood. So if we all show up, they should be open to talking."

"So where are they now, Pops?" Bradley asked.

"When they were down at the community center, they told me they like to hang out at a park over here," my dad began. "Now we may encounter many people, not just the people I represented. Anything can pop off, so be ready. You all know your positions, gifts, and what to do."

Yeah, I just heal everybody once my dad and brothers are done fighting them. We finally pulled up to the park my dad was talking about. There must have been about 30 people in this park. All Black males, ages ranging from 14-28. My dad kept a forcefield around the car after we exited. My dad walked up to the 30 guys. He had us hidden in a forcefield until it was time for us to be unleashed. About 15 of them had their guns drawn, and the rest of them just stood ready. One guy stood in front of all of them. I guess he was their leader, Haine, who my dad heard about from the kids. Haine was a rapper and gang member from Englewood. He was about 5‘11, with twists in his hair, and brown skin. He had many tattoos, but what stood out to me the most were the two tear drops under one eye, and one under the other. He also had a bunch of other tattoos all over him. He looked to be about 27. He spoke while everyone else stood ready to shoot or fight.

"Well if it ain't Chicago's finest superhero. Seems like you missing ya finest one. Where is the Nubian goddess? And those kids?" Haine walked up to my dad.

"They're out sick, but I'm still on the job. How'd y'all get all of these guns?" my dad asked.

"Why you worried about it?" Haine asked.

"Because these guns are killing innocent kids and people in Chicago. I ain't havin it," my dad asserted.

Haine started laughing. "Man these guns have always been around. This is just how it is in Chiraq, ain't you heard?

We ain't the only ones with guns in Chicago, so why you comin' at us?" Haine asked.

"Look, I don't want any trouble. I just want to know where you're getting the guns," my dad responded.

Haine stepped close to my dad with a frown on his face. "Look, I see y'all on the news. How you try not to kill anybody — but we killers out here on these streets. And when you run your mouth, you end up dead. It's life or death out here, and I'm just trying to make this bread. If I tell you where I get my guns, I have no protection. You gon' come out here and protect me? Once you take my guns, you take my product, and if you take my product, you take my money. You gon' give me a job?"

"It doesn't have to be like this..." my dad began to say.

"Nigga it's always been like this. You got yo powers and I got mine. You got yo crew and I got mine. And ain't none of us telling you nothing about the guns."

"What if I told you we could help you out of this?"

"Bro that's trash, ain't no comin' out of these streets."

"Exactly. Aren't you tired of this? Aren't you tired of having to look over your shoulder. Aren't you tired of your crew dying? Aren't you tired of kids dying? Aren't you tired of this war with your own people over nothing?"

"These people that I kill not my people. And this war ain't over nothing. It's over life. I gotta do what I gotta do, and with me getting mine, some people might get hurt along the way. That's just how it is. I ain't none of you. But what I wanna ask — who told you where we be at? How you know about our spot?"

"No one did, we heard around. I don't know any of these kids personally."

"Yeah, aight." Haine turned around, and at that moment a few of Haine's crew shot at my dad, but he had made himself bulletproof. He opened up the forcefield, and we all ran out. Bradley and Calhoun started to fight the guys. Lena started moving fast with a strong rope that Saff gave us to tie everyone up. Calhoun pulled the rope to lift them all up, and make them all drop. He threw them into the air and back down again. That got rid of about ten. Ali and I started fighting some of the members who didn't have guns pulled out. These were some of the kids we saved, so they didn't fight back much. They were just trying not to be seen faking it by their crew. We went easy on them. Bradley had been practicing his gifts and knew how to shoot from his skeleton now. He would shoot different people in the legs from his hands as his skin faded away. The guys were confused as to how Bradley could absorb and shoot bullets. My dad was able to run fast like Lena, life people like Cal, and become bullet-proof like Bradley. I would heal everyone once we were done. Finally, only three kids were left. The ones that Ali and I were fighting. They led us further into the park so no one would see us. It was really dark in the park. While my little sister, big brothers, and dad were still fighting, Ali and I asked the kids questions.

“Okay, so who is giving you guys the guns?” Ali asked

“Y’all not gon’ tell where you got this information we give you, right?” one of the guys asked.

“No. And what are y’all doing out here? We thought y’all were helping out at the community center owned by your lawyer?” I asked them.

“Like Haine said, it’s hard out here in these streets and you don’t get out that easy,” one of the other guys said.

“Well, what do you guys need from us? What can we do to help you?” Ali asked.

“Nothing. We giving you this information because we believe you can help. Y’all give us hope. Out here on these streets there is no hope. We know you can change things,” one of the guys said.

“So what names do you have?” I asked.

“The guy we know, where we get the guns and drugs from, his name is Arakunrin. I don’t know where he gets the guns from, but he supplies us with everything," one of the guys said.

"Do you know where we can find him?" Ali asked.

"He usually stops by every couple of weeks. With another guy with a name we don't remember. Everyone calls him K," he said again.

"Just K?" I asked.

"Yeah. Oh and he has the word breed on his shirt every time he comes over," another guy said.

"They should be coming back again pretty soon," another one of the kids said.

"Thank you, we won't let you guys down. We'll have to pretend you passed out here. We will heal everyone so no one will have any bruises, and they won't suspect a thing. The police chief will be here soon. He'll let you all go, but probably not some of those guys who shot at our leader. So they won't be around for a while," Ali said.

“Do y’all do this because y’all want to or because y’all have to?” one of them asked us.

“What do you mean?” I asked.

“This superhero thing. Do y’all do this because y’all want to or because y’all have to?” I didn’t say anything. That’s when Ali said,

“A little bit of both. What about y’all?”

“The same thing, both,” one of them said.

“I don’t want to do this at all,” another one said.

“I kinda have to do this. It’s a family thing,” the last one said.

“How old are you guys?” Ali asked.

“I’m 15, he is too, and he’s 13,” one of them answered.

“We’re 15 and 13 too.”

“Y’ALL LET'S GO, IT’S TIME!” Ali and I heard Bradley yell in the distance.

“Alright, lay down right here. If anyone asks you anything, say we knocked you out cold. Throw your guns over there to make it look like we knocked them out of your hands," Ali told them.

"Thank y'all. What do y'all call each other? Like, you know, your superhero names?" the 13 year old asked us. "Superheroes are my favorite, that's why I ask."

"We don't have superhero names, but we have a collective name. We're the Splendid Saba." Ali said.

"Splendid Saba?" one of them asked, looking confused.

"Yeah, because it's seven of us. Saba means seven. So we're the Splendid Seven," I said.

"Alright guys, we gotta go. Lay down and don't tell anyone anything. Not even when you go to the community center," Ali said.

They laid down and one of them asked,

"Hey, how y'all know so much about us? Did our lawyer talk to y'all?"

"Kind of," I said as Ali and I ran away.

The police chief came with the CPD and arrested everyone. My dad told them about the kids who gave us the information and to keep them safe. Ali told the chief that they gave the information we needed to know. My dad, brothers, and Lena had all of the guys tied up. About 15 cops came in and put everyone in handcuffs. I healed all of the other members' wounds. We all got back into our invisible truck, and while in the car, the chief called us, and so did Mama. We changed back into our own clothes using the bracelet Saffore gave us. Dad took the forcefield off when we were close to home. Uncle Saffore had installed some cool gadgets in our car and we were able to pull up a holographic image of the chief and Mama.

"So Sly, what information did y'all get?" the chief asked us as we drove home.

"Ali and Wil got the information. You know me, Lena, Cal, and B don't have the gift of communication. Not as much as Ali, Wil, and my wife. We wouldn't get any information without them," my dad said. Maybe this is what I was good for. Maybe it helps when people aren't afraid of you. When you aren't looked at as a threat, maybe they're comfortable with sharing things with you.

"Well we talked to some of the kids from your community center, Daddy. They told us the supplier of the guns is this guy named Arakunrin and the other guy is named K," Ali started.

"Arakunrin and K?" my mama asked.

"Yeah Ma, they did tell us that the guy named K always wears a t-shirt with the word breed on it," Ali said.

"Great, so now we have to figure out who this K and Arakunrin are," the chief said.

"You guys were over there for a while, what were y'all talking to them about?" Bradley asked.

"They told us that they gave us the information because we give them hope. And there is no hope on the streets. They also told us that they don't enjoy doing this. And we told them what would happen to them," I said.

"Yeah, they also asked if we had superhero names. I just told them that our name is collective. We're the Splendid Saba," I said.

"It might be cool if we had our own names. Like me being Ferocious Five." Cal said.

"Yeah, that would be cool," Bradley said.

"Excuse me, Daddy, can I tell you something?" Lena said.

"Yes baby, what's wrong?" my dad said.

"Daddy, a lot of the guys had tattoos that looked a lot like the symbol that was on the monster that we fought for Bradley," Lena said.

"What monster did y'all fight for Bradley, Sly?" the chief asked.

"This monster was a racial hatred monster, Chief. It was those kids that we told you about who Bradley had been with. They combined to create a monster when we fought them. So Lena, you're saying the tattoo on the members looked like the image that was on the monster? And what was it on the monster? Was it a tattoo as well?"

"I don't know. It looked like a tattoo on the monster. It was on his arm. It looked like something in Hebrew."

"Good job, baby girl using that eidetic memory," Mama said.

"Thank you, Mommy!" Lena said, smiling.

"So maybe those guys, Kuzaliana, Taifa, and Chuki, are connected to Arakunrin and K?" Ali said.

"Maybe it is them?" Cal suggested. "Remember they said they take on different forms to spread hatred."

"Wait, you guys fought against a racial hatred monster and didn't tell me?" the chief asked.

"Well Chief, you never asked how we found Bradley," my dad said.

"Chief, we don't tell you everything. Some battles the CPD can't fight. Like racial hatred monsters." my mama said.

"This is true. This is why I called y'all. So what do y'all think?" the chief asked.

"We don't know," my dad said, and everyone got quiet.

"Wait, Wil?" Bradley said. I looked up at him.

"You said that Chuki means hatred, Kuzaliana means breed, and Taifa means nation, all in Swahili, right?" Bradley asked me.

"Right?" I shrugged.

"So the guy named K could be Kuzaliana, which means breed. His name has a K and he always has the word breed on his shirt," Bradley went on.

"That could be true, Bradley," my mom started out. "But who is Arakunrin?" she asked.

"I don't know. Wil, is Arakunrin Swahili for something?"

"No, Arakunrin is Yoruba for brother," I explained. "Yoruba is a West African language, and Swahili is East African."

"YES!" Bradley said excitedly. "Pops, you said to Haine that they're fighting a war against their own people. Killing their own children. I spent enough time with these guys to know that all of them represent hatred. Arakunrin and Kuzaliana supplying the guns to the guys in gangs represents hatred against your brother. Or hatred against those who are the same breed as you because they kill other Black people in the same neighborhood. The guys think they're fighting a war against a rival gang member here in Chicago, but it's all hatred. Self-hatred, hatred against your brother, hatred against your own breed. And breed was a racial slur as well for Black people. Because Black people were seen as property like cattle during slavery, and their children were born as property. Or bred as property like cattle."

"I get it, Bradley, I get it. Splendid job, Son. So if we find Arakunrin that might lead us to Kuzaliana. If we can beat them we can potentially stop the gun violence here in Englewood. And even if we can't stop it, we'll be able to slow it down," my dad said.

"You see! You see how all of you worked together to figure that out. This is why our family is splendid! It took all of you working together. All of your communication, healing, brain power, and connection to understand that. SPLENDID JOB EVERYONE!" my mama said.

"Thanks, Ma. Have you solved anything at the CPD?" Bradley asked.

"Well baby, with how y'all brains were working, I'm sure we would've figured it out a long time ago. But there are so many people here that I have to get to know and who have to trust me. My intuition helps me to see when someone is lying, but it doesn't make them tell me the truth. But I can say I don't think it's just a brotherhood of cops who are doing this. I think it's someone higher up. And if you all find that Arakunrin is connected to Kuzaliana, someone within the CPD may be connected to that racial hatred monster as well," my mama explained.

"So did they tell y'all where Kuzaliana and Arakunrin are?" the chief asked.

"They told us that they come to the park every two weeks to drop off new supplies. So they should be coming next weekend," Ali said.

"Perfect, we'll be back then," my dad said.

"Mommy, can you join us to fight them?" Lena asked.

"Yes, baby. I can join you all for that night. I feel that once we've tackled that part of the monster, we can focus on the CPD more. Then we can find out what's going on at headquarters," my mom responded proudly.

We were all proud of what we did that night. We got closer to solving the problem of gun and gang violence in Chicago. Now we just had to fight it. Uncle Saffore did tell us that this problem was bigger than what we thought. We went back to the apartment and went to sleep. And woke up the next day ready to train with Uncle Saffore for our fight that weekend.

CHAPTER 2 - BROKEN BONES AND BROKEN HOMES

My mom was still at Headquarters, and my dad was working on some stuff for his job. Some lawyer stuff I guess. He didn't feel comfortable leaving us home alone in Englewood. So during the day when he had to work, he would take us to the lab with Uncle Saff to keep us busy. While there, Uncle Saff would help us strengthen our gifts and understand them more. He would also help us to understand the gadgets he made for us as well. He would tell us how our bracelets would help us change from our superhero clothes to regular clothes, talk to each other, record information, and pull up a holographic image of each other when we called one another. Stuff we already knew. But then he also told us they could share information with one another. So when we sent a message the whole family could see it. Like a group chat. Since Uncle Saffore was helping us train with fighting and strengthening our gifts, I wanted to know if there was a way that we could also have weapons. Bradley had his bullets, Cal had his super strength, and my dad had force fields and the ability to take on our gifts. All of that they could use to protect themselves. But I didn't have anything like that. I needed something to protect myself.

"Alright nieces and nephews, I have a few things planned for each of you today. Ali, we'll start with you. I'm going to show you some more traumatic experiences, and I want you to focus on blocking them out. We're going to work on your breathing and blocking technique," Uncle Saff explained to Ali.

"Got it!" Ali responded.

"Bradley, we're going to work more on your aim with your shooting. Now the bullets can come out of your body from many different parts. Your hands, your shoulder blades, knee caps, and shoulders. We're going to work on that. We're also going to work on your aim with your hands since you told me that your bullets sometimes go to the left when you use your hands," Uncle Saff explained to Bradley.

"Dope Unc!" Bradley said.

"Lena, since you travel as fast as the speed of light, I've realized that there are some gifts you won't have yet. But there may be things that we can start working on now to see if they may pop up a little bit. Every child is different and goes through puberty at different times. There may be some things with you that can develop now, even though you haven't gone through puberty. Light can take the form of radio waves, microwaves, x-rays, gamma rays, ultraviolet light, and infrared light. This means you may be able to use your gifts to heat things, to hear things, to create images, and see past what the regular human eye sees. We may not be able to find out today, but give it time, niecy wiecy," Uncle Saff explained to Allena.

"That sounds so cool!" Lena said.

"Calhoun, for you we'll focus on pushing your strength while in pain like we did last time. Last time it was 1,000 pounds. Today we'll go to 2,000, and I'll use the pain inflictor," Uncle Saff explained to Cal.

"Ready, Unc!" Cal said.

"And Wil, we are going to focus on you strengthening your ability to heal new wounds permanently and heal wounds that one is born with. We're also going to focus on strengthening your linguistic ability. I'll introduce you to some native languages and dialects that have been lost. Especially from Native American tribes and our ancestors during the transatlantic slave trade," Uncle Saff explained to me.

"Sounds great." I decided I'd ask him about the weapons after training.

Our training went well. Bradley was able to aim better with his hands that day. He was still trying to figure out how to shoot bullets accurately from other parts of his body and isolate the shooting in those parts. Cal was able to keep the 2,000 pound weight lifted until the pain inflictor was up to about six. Ali was able to block out what she saw after crying for two minutes. She beat her record. Usually she has a panic attack for quite some time before she can calm down. Lena was able to create heat with her running, even without going through puberty. I was able to reverse the damage on a kidney that Uncle Saffore had. And I learned 17 new dialects. Some from the West African region and some from Native American tribes. Even though it was hard work, we all understood that in order to become better heroes we had to understand our gifts more and strengthen them. It scared us to see what we were capable of sometimes, but that fear only drove us to become better. Everyone was getting ready to go get in the car with Dad, so I stayed back and asked what I had been wanting to ask all day.

“Hey Unc, can I ask you something?”

“Sure nephew, what's wrong?” Uncle Saff asked.

“Do you think you can make me a weapon with your science?”

“What?”

“Like something I can use during battle with the monster?”

“Why do you want that, nephew?”

“Well, it’s because Bradley has his gift to absorb bullets and shoot them. Cal is super strong. My dad creates force fields and has the power to mimic our abilities. All of them are fighters, but I’m not. They have to protect me when we fight. I’m known as the gentle one who talks to people, who calms them, and who heals them. But what if my dad, Wil, and B aren’t around? What do I have?”

"Sit down, nephew," Uncle Saff said to me as we sat on a bench inside his lab. "Now look around. What do you see?"

"Your lab."

"Now look at me. What do you see?"

"I see you."

"Am I super strong? Do I have a weapon? Can I absorb bullets, or mimic everyone's abilities?"

"No."

"You see, nephew, being superhuman doesn't always mean being a fighter. Some of us are given gifts from God that aren't about fighting. You are a strong fighter. Not as strong as Cal, or your dad, or Bradley, but you have something that they don't. You have gifts that they don't. You can heal others, and you can understand them. Sometimes the greatest gift, the greatest superpower, is connection, love, solidarity, and healing. Look at how the kids were comfortable with telling you and Ali how they felt, and telling you what they knew. You were able to build trust. And just like all of your family can use their powers for bad, you can too. When someone trusts you and you betray that trust, you can really break them. So your gift is still strong, it's still important, and it can still be used as a weapon. That's what makes it powerful. My gifts are the same. I can create with my ability. I can understand with my ability. I can counsel. I can train. I can push you all to the next level. That's a superpower. So I won't be making a weapon for you, as I haven't for any of your siblings. But I will train you to develop your powers to the best of their ability."

"I understand Unc, and thank you!"

"You're welcome! Oh, and nephew there is nothing wrong with being gentle. Girls love it!" Uncle Saff said with a look of satisfaction on his face. I had to think about what he said, and he was right. I didn't have to have a weapon in order to be a great superhero. Sometimes the power to de-escalate a problem by talking to someone in a language they understand or healing a person's wounds is a superpower all on its own. Once we were done, I ran to the car.

"Wil, Son, what took you so long?" my dad asked.

"Oh, I just had to talk to Uncle Saff about my training for next time," I said to my dad.

"Okay, good!"

It was later on in the day. My dad had cooked, and we had eaten dinner. I missed many things about my mom, but I definitely missed her home cooked meals. My dad wasn't the worst cook, but he definitely wasn't as good as my mom. My mom decided to call us and talk to us one on one so we could tell her what was wrong. And if we didn't tell everything, of course Ali would. She was the closest to mom, besides Lena, and was always around her. Then she got to me.

"Hey Ma!" I said.

"Hey my sweet boy, how are you feeling?" My mom asked.

"I'm okay. I was able to talk to Uncle Saff today."

"Oh yeah? About what?"

"About making me a weapon." She had a concerned look on her face.

"You mean building you a weapon or turning you into a weapon?"

"No, like physically making a weapon for me to use during battle."

"Why would you want that?"

"Well I told him that I've been feeling like, as a man…"

"Wait, so you're a man now?"

"Yeah Ma, I'm thirteen." She had a smirk on her face like she was laughing at me on the inside.

"Okay, go on," she said.

"As a man, I'm not a fighter like Dad, Cal, and B."

"But baby, that's what makes you special."

"I know, and that's what Uncle Saff told me. He also told me girls love nice guys."

"Yeah, I can say that this is true. But also sweetheart, being a fighter doesn't make you masculine. In fact, that's a toxic view of masculinity," she told me.

"What do you mean?"

"Baby, being a man isn't just about fighting people. What your brothers and father do isn't just fighting, they protect. And they protect because they care."

"Yeah, but Ma, I'm not a good runner or baseball player like B and Cal."

"No, you're not. You're artistic, and creative. And who says that men can't be those things?"

"I guess no one."

"Baby, we all have different talents and different gifts. And there isn't just one way to be a man. Being a man means having different ways of protecting the ones you love. You can de-escalate situations — imagine if the cops did this, or people in the military, or teachers in school. Imagine how many people's lives would be saved. You have the ability to do that. Baby, we have a lot of fighters in this world, but there aren't very many people who can heal wounds, physically and mentally. Our world is full of broken people, and your gift, my gift, Ali's gift, and Saffore's gift allows us to heal people. That's what makes it so special. Healing is a power that Jesus showed his disciples. The ability to speak so all could understand is something that happened when the Holy Ghost came upon the disciples. Your gift comes from God, and you're able to do both. And you're able to heal those your brother may shoot. And where would Cal be without you? And your dad can create force fields around people to protect them, which was his original super power. He wasn't much of a fighter either. It was something that developed over time. He was actually more of a nerd. And he didn't have many muscles when I first met him, like he does now. But he does a lot fighting in the courtroom to protect the children he represents. You understand?"

"Yeah, Ma."

"Gentleness and love are superpowers, don't ever forget that. It doesn't show weakness, it actually shows a lot of strength."

"I love you, Ma!"

"I love you too, baby! I'll be with you all this weekend to join you in the fight against hatred."

My mom and Uncle Saff made me feel better about my gifts. If I wasn't a healer or the dopest communicator, I wouldn't be able to connect with people, heal people, and love them. We were all done talking to my mom. Ali was combing Lena's hair. Bradley was lifting weights. Cal was writing some lyrics. Dad was getting some work done. I was drawing everyone in action while we all watched television in the living room.

"So kids, how did training go today?" my dad asked.

"It went good, Daddy. I have a new superpower. I can move super fast and create heat. Uncle Saff is trying to see if

I have new powers connected to light since I'm able to run faster than the speed of light," Lena started off.

"That's awesome, baby girl! Look at you learning new superpowers already. You'll be able to cook soon, and we won't need an oven. We'll just use you," my dad said, and Lena started laughing.

"Ali?" my dad said.

"It went great, Dad. I was able to calm myself down with breathing. I stopped crying in two minutes and blocked what I just saw. Beating my time. And Uncle Saffore told me to hold Lena's hand whenever I'm sad. She always has beautiful and happy thoughts, and that helps to calm me," Ali explained.

"That's beautiful, Bay Bay! Baby girl, look at you helping your sister. I love how you're using your abilities to help one another. Speaking of helping one another, let's talk about the Stanton twins," my dad said.

“Well, I was able to lift 2,000 pounds while Uncle Saff used the pain inflictor. It lasted until the inflictor was on number six. So I’m getting stronger, even while experiencing sickle cell pain,” Cal said.

“Splendid Samson! Wil, son?” my dad said.

“Well, you all will probably find out soon. But I asked Uncle Saff to make a weapon for me.” Everyone stopped what they were doing and looked at me.

“Bro, why would you want a weapon?” Cal asked me

“Well, I was feeling like less of a man…” I began.

“Wait, so because you’re thirteen you’re a man now?” Ali asked.

“Mama said the same thing. Yeah, Cal and I are men, we're thirteen now,” I explained to her.

“Boy, bye,” Ali said as she waved her hand.

“Ali, don't interrupt. Wil, son, why did you want a weapon?” my dad asked.

"Because Dad, you, Cal, and B are all fighters and I'm not. You all have to protect me, and I want to be able to protect myself and others," I explained to them.

"But Wil, we don't mind protecting you," Bradley told me.

"I know. And Mom and Uncle Saff helped me realize that healing and communication are superpowers. Sometimes they speak louder than fists," I responded.

"That's right. Wil, son, I wasn't always a great fighter or athlete," my dad said.

"And that's what mom told me and there is nothing wrong with gentleness. And masculinity doesn't mean fighting or hurting others."

"Right, and Wil, son, listen to me. Bradley, Cal, and I don't fight because we want to hurt people or be seen as frightening. People are afraid enough of us as Black guys, so that's not what we're trying to do. We fight because we have to. You have the ability to get people to trust you, and not everybody has that," my dad said.

"I understand. And I realize that my superpower is just as important as anyone else's in this family," I assured my dad.

"I know it is for me. Where would I be without you?" Cal said.

"Where would we all be without you? The power to heal is important for all of us. Well, maybe not Bradley because he doesn't get hurt. But think about Uncle Saffore. He's not a fighter, but he helps so many people, including us," Ali said.

"Yeah, and he told me this as well," I said.

"Son, don't ever doubt how strong and important your ability is. None of you. Your abilities, although confusing and difficult, are something to be completely proud of," my dad said, "They're all gifts from God."

I loved that my family was focused on cheering me up because I felt so bad before talking to them. I realize that there is strength in gentleness and power in communication.

"Alright kids, let's get ready for bed. We have a big weekend ahead of us in the next few days," my dad said as he put his things away so we could all get ready for bed.

CHAPTER 3 - ALLEVIATE THE HATRED

"So Wil how you feel?" Cal asked me as we were suiting up to head out tonight. It was finally the weekend when Arakunrin and K would be dropping off supplies for Haine and his crew. I wonder if they'll be surprised that Haine isn't there.

"I feel good, I'm ready for tonight," I told Cal.

"Aight, remember we need you. If you weren't able to heal, our work as superheroes wouldn't be the same."

"I know Cal, thanks man!"

"Alright, everyone ready? Your mom is almost here," Dad said.

"Is Mommy going to ride in the car with us?" Lena asked.

"Yeah, we're all going to go together. Hopefully after doing this we'll be able to find out some more information on her end at headquarters," Dad said.

"I hope so, I'm tired of being in this little bitty apartment," Bradley said.

"We know, you say it, like, every day," Lena said. We all laughed, and B picked her up and tickled her. A message came in from Mom on all of our bracelets.

Downstairs.

"Alright everyone, this is it. We may see these same dudes we saw before when we fought the racial hatred monster. Bradley, will you be okay?" my dad asked.

"Of course, Pops, I'll be fine," Bradley told him.

"Okay, remember the plan and everything should go smoothly," my dad said.

Inside the truck my dad created a force field around us as we drove back to the park.

"So Dad, we locked the guys up. So who's going to be at the park?" I asked.

"Wil, Son, those were just the gang members that were out there that night. But they're not the only gang members. Some of their other members will be out there tonight. Or rival members will be coming to take over since Haine is locked up," my dad explained.

"Got it!" I said.

We pulled up to the park, and sure enough there were about 20 guys there along with some of the kids that we didn't see last time. We waited in our car for an hour. Just when we thought that Arakunrin and K weren't coming tonight, they pulled up. We had never seen Arakunrin before, but K was definitely Kuzaliana. Only he looked a bit different. He didn't look like a high schooler anymore. He had a beard, and more weight on him. He looked a lot older. We were able to tell by his eyes.

"B, is that Kuzaliana?" Ali asked.

"Yup, that's him," Bradley reassured us. "He may have taken on a different form, but I have a feeling that's him."

"Do you think Arakunrin is a part of the monster like them or a regular human?" Ali asked.

"I don't know, you'll be able to tell when you get close to him," Bradley said.

"Alright then, let's go," my dad said as he was about to get out of the car.

"Wait, Dad. I think we should wait," Bradley said.

"What do you mean?" My mom asked.

"I think we shouldn't fight here — it'll be expected," Bradley said. "I'm sure they've heard already that we were here. So I think when they get back in their car, we should follow them. We may be able to see where they're staying and get some new information."

"Good idea, son!" my dad said. The force field was still around us, so we pulled up closer so we could hear what they were talking about.

"So where is Haine? I ain't never seen you before," Arakunrin asked the new leader.

"Haine got locked up last week with some more of our crew. I'm Karahia, fillin' in for him while he's gone."

"What happened to Haine? I been knowing him since he was real young," Kuzaliana said.

"Man, those superheroes came out. Had a fight with about 30 of our dudes. Annihilated them, and then the chief came and put them away," Karachi's explained.

"What superheroes?" Arakunrin asked.

"You know, Chicago's finest superheroes. I guess they're called the Splendid Saba," Karahia said.

"Have they been back?" Kuzaliana asked.

"Naw, not since then."

"Did one of them absorb bullets?" Kuzaliana asked.

"Oh yeah, and shot 'em out too. But what was odd was the lady wasn't with them. I don't know where she was at."

"Arakunrin, we gotta go," Kuzaliana said.

"Alright, here's your stuff. Thanks for the information," Arakunrin said to Karahia. Arakunrin and Kuzaliana got in the car and started to drive away. We followed them all the way to a place in Indiana. It looked like it was just a house. But then we looked through the windows and saw them open a wall and put in a code to a room that led down some stairs. Lena was able to remember the code. Cal tore the door from its hinges, and once inside, Lena put the code in, and we all went down the stairs. Dad made us invisible the entire time by putting a force field around us. While we were downstairs we realized that this must be one of their lairs. We saw images of evil dictators, killers who committed genocide, and a slew of different images representing hatred. We figured that these must be different people throughout history whose forms they were able to take on. Or who they were able to get hatred into. No one was down here, just Arakunrin and Kuzaliana. Then we heard a conversation between the two of them.

"We need Haine back. He was doing a fantastic job leading everybody. A lot of hatred was spreading around. So many people were shot and killed under his watch," Arakunrin said.

"I know. I trained him myself. Came around when he was young and recruited him. He was willing and ready to be a part of the gang. I don't know about this new guy," Kuzaliana said.

"Why don't you call the police superintendent tomorrow to see if Haine can be released?" Arakunrin asked.

"Yeah, I'mma do that. I keep feeling like those superheroes will be back," Kuzaliana said. Just then, my dad removed the force field from around us.

"Miss me?" Bradley asked.

Just then, he shot both guys in the shoulders and legs. After that, Cal picked them up by the collar and held them up against the wall. They were bleeding. We hadn't known that they could even be hurt. I mean, they were monsters, after all.

"How did y'all get here?" Kuzaliana asked.

"Who are these people? Are these the superheroes they were talking about?" Arakunrin asked.

"Yeah, and that's Bradley. We go way back," Kuzaliana said.

"Keep my name out yo mouth, bro" Bradley told him.

"And tell us what you know about the superintendent," my dad said.

"We don't know nothing," Arakunrin said. Bradley shot him in the other leg.

"Alright, enough of this," Kuzaliana said. They held hands and combined to create a monster. While they were changing, Cal wasn't able to hold them down anymore. Their monster was not as big as the one we fought before, and this time it was wounded. Images of all of the black and white pictures we saw on the wall formed its body now. They were connected by one arm and one leg. So the monster had two outer legs and arms, and one middle leg and arm. With its three fists it started to fight. It punched Cal and sent him flying through a wall to the backyard. Bradley kept shooting at it, the gunshots seeming to slow it down. Cal came back through the wall and my dad mimicked some of Cal's super strength so he and Cal could fight the monster together. Four hands were better than three, I guess that monster learned today that it wasn't the only one who had hands. It started getting tired. My mom had taught Ali how to jump high in the air and kick, and together they kicked both of the monsters' heads. My mom kicked one, and Ali kicked the other. Once it became dizzy from the kick, tired from the fight, and losing some of its monster blood from the bullets, Lena started running around the monster, and with her newfound power, created a flame around him. As it began to burn and disintegrate it said,

"You'll never beat this. We've been here forever and we're stronger than you'll ever know." Bradley shot at it.

With that shot it died and disintegrated in Lena's flames and nothing but ashes were left. We called the fire department after the house burned to ashes. My dad started driving back to Chicago to drop my mom back off at her hotel, and on our drive back to Chicago, we started talking about what we'd heard. So we called the chief.

"Chief, we have some new information," my dad started out.

"Alright, I was waiting for you all to call me. I thought you wanted me and my team to come out," the chief responded

"Well, Bradley came up with a brilliant plan that we should follow Arakunrin and Kuzaliana. So we waited it out, and they led us to a house in Indiana," My mom said,

“What did you find?” the chief asked.

“Chief, get this. Arakunrin and Kuzaliana mentioned the superintendent. They wouldn’t tell us what they knew, but they said they would call him to get Haine released from prison,” Ali said.

“For real?” the chief asked, his holographic image looking confused.

“Yes!” My mom told him.

“That makes sense, there have been times my guys put away different gang members and the superintendent instantly let them go. It was also the superintendent who didn’t want to fire the crooked cops or the cops that shot innocent, unarmed Black people. The cops only have to step down because of the public protest.”

“So what are we going to do?” Cal asked.

“Well I’ll be at headquarters next week,” my mom said. “The superintendent will be in for meetings. Chief, do you think I can join you all during those meetings?”

"Of course you can. I'll be there as well, so I'll introduce you as my new assistant. Make sure you wear your disguise so they can't recognize you. If these guys are connected like you think they are, you may be fighting someone you've fought before," the chief said.

"Ma, he also said that this thing is bigger than what we think. Do you think they mean that it goes past the superintendent?" Ali asked.

"I think so, baby. America is a huge place so I'm sure that there are more hate monsters everywhere. But we can at least take care of the ones in Chicago first."

"So since we defeated this hate monster, what do you think this means?" Cal asked.

"I don't know, I guess we'll have to find out," my dad said.

We had taken the force field off the car and changed back into our regular clothes. We dropped my mom off at her hotel and rode home. It was late and we were tired. Dad decided to take the day off tomorrow and we all decided to stay in. We didn't go see Uncle Saffore. We thought it would be nice to have a family outing, so the next day we picked up Mom and rode along the river at Navy Pier. It was nice. It had been a long time since we did something together as a family.

"So Ma, what's the plan? How are you going to get information from the superintendent? And when will you want us to join you?" Ali asked while we were on our boat ride.

"Well the chief said I'll be acting as his assistant. He's going to try to schedule some meetings with the superintendent at his house, and I'll be able to come. That way I can come and see if I can pick up on anything or find any new information. If Arakunrin mentioned the superintendent that means that someone within the CPD is connected to them," my mom explained.

"You don't think it's the Superintendent?" Bradley asked.

"No baby. Just like Haine isn't a part of the monster but is a part of the hatred, I believe that the superintendent is a human spewing hatred. I don't think he's a part of the monster," my assured us.

"So if he's not a part of the monster, and we may have to fight the monster, how do we figure out who's connected to the superintendent?" Ali asked.

"I don't know, baby, but we'll find out soon," my mom said.

The next week, the time was approaching for Mom to meet with the superintendent. She called us and told us to turn on the news.

"Well, Chicago has some great news. It seems that the gun violence has subsided quite a bit. Usually summers in Chicago bring high numbers of gun violence incidents, resulting in the killing and shooting of innocent victims. This week and weekend, there have only been two shootings, and no one died in either shooting. We are hoping that this trend stays," the newscaster said.

"Wow, I never thought I'd see the day when we'd watch the Chicago news and no one was shot and killed," my dad said. "Praise God!"

"Do you think this happened because we defeated Arakunrin and Kuzaliana?" I asked.

"Yes, but don't put your guard down just because this is happening. Remember they said this goes higher than what we think. If Arakunrin was a part of the monster, there could be more, and they could be coming. But I think by defeating Kuzaliana we stopped a big part of the monster," my dad said.

"That's dope!" Bradley said.

"Dad, wait, turn up the volume," Ali said.

"Even though gun violence went down in Black and Brown neighborhoods this week, a video has surfaced showing the killing of two unarmed, Black teenagers in North Lawndale. They died at the hands of the CPD officers. Another similar incident happened in Chatham. Protesters have been marching in the area, and activists had this to say…"

"Mama has to move quick," Bradley said.

"Yeah, I wonder if us defeating Kuzaliana made the rest of the monster stronger or more angrier since the gun violence has slowed down?" Cal said.

"I'm sure the rest of the monster knows by now, and I'm sure it's angry. I hope we can find out who's close to the superintendent or if it is him so we can finish this job," my dad said.

PART 5: MOTHER KNOWS BEST

CHAPTER 1 - INTUITION

"So Vivian — I mean, Veronica — what is the plan for today? I have to remember to use your undercover name," the chief started to ask.

"I'll be coming in with you to the meeting as your assistant. While in the meeting, I'll be able to get a feel for the superintendent. So sit close by him, and I'll sit in between you all to be close to him. I'll use the system here to look into the background of the superintendent," I told the chief.

“Well there is no need to do that. We’ve looked over his background before he was assigned as superintendent. He worked his way up in the police department and became the superintendent,” the chief assured me.

“How much do you all know about his personal life or childhood?”

“We don’t know a lot. He’s a very private man.”

“What if you had a dinner party and invited him? Do you think he’d attend?”

“He might. Why do you ask?”

“Maybe we can learn some new information about him. Something to connect the dots. You see the guy Haine that you recently locked up had known Kuzaliana since he was a child. They had gotten close to Haine just like they were trying to get close to Bradley. If we can talk to the superintendent we may be able to find out who’s close to him and who is helping him spread hatred within the department.”

"That's an idea. Maybe find out who he's close to. Best friend, companion, mentor, something like that?"

"Exactly."

"His 30-year anniversary as superintendent will be coming up in a couple of weeks. I'll throw him a small dinner party at the hotel where you're staying. What if Alicia comes to the dinner party?" The chief asked.

"Why would Alicia come?" I asked the chief.

"She could shake his hand and find some things out about him."

"That's a good idea. Okay, she can come to the dinner party. I'm sure she'll enjoy spending some alone time with me. She's been calling me the most out of the kids. Except for Lena, of course"

"Sounds like a plan. I'll see you at headquarters."

Being a mom was the best job. It was nice to take a little break from the family, something I hadn't done in a while, but I was always worried about my kids. It was not just because I was a mother or because I was intuitive. Honestly, being intuitive was an added bonus. But being a mom of five Black children with superpowers was unsettling. I know every mother feels guilty at some point, but I always felt guilty that because Sylvester and I weren't careful, we brought something to our kids that they didn't want. My kids enjoyed being superheroes, but I always worried that this superhero thing would be what hurt them in the end. The fear that they had, the uncertainty with their identity and purpose. Just the other day when I talked to all of them, Ali told me how she was always unsure of her own feelings because she could feel everyone else's. Bradley told me how he was still mourning the loss of Ahava, feeling guilty about not being able to save him. And feeling stupid because he had sided with the same guys that we were trying to defeat.

Cal told me he felt horrible about having sickle cell and didn't want to have it forever. I always felt so bad that me and my husband's genes were what passed this onto him. I knew this bothered him. He was my only baby who was sick, so I always felt that I had to pay him a little more attention. Wil felt inadequate because he was my gentle boy and not a fighter like the other males in our family. And I felt guilty because Lena missed me so much and cried every night when I called her. I had to stay on the phone with her in order for her to go to sleep. Our family was not normal. It bothered me so much as a mom that I did this to my children. When I was younger and first found out that I had superpowers, I hated it. I hated knowing when someone was lying, or knowing that something bad was about to happen. But I loved knowing how to figure out complex systems and problems easily. Other than that, I felt so weird. I never told anyone about my abilities so no one knew except Sylvester and Saffore knew for the longest time. I was glad that my kids, especially Ali, had a friend to confide in about this superhero thing. I knew for me, it would've made life so much easier if I had a girlfriend who knew what I was going through and was still my friend regardless of my abnormalities.

What's a mother to do? I hoped that understanding them, acknowledging their pain, responding to it, and giving them the best advice was enough. What I did love about my ability was that my children could never lie to me. Every mother's dream. Even if I didn't know everything about how they felt or what they were doing, I could always ask Ali. She was my girl, she told me everything. My husband was a huge help too. Whenever I felt like this, doubting everything, it always helped to call my husband. Sylvester always knew what to say and helped me calm down my worries about all of this. He loved being a superhero, so where he was ambitious about our superhero missions, I was a bit more reserved. We balanced each other in that way. It had always been like that ever since we were in college together. He would get me to take more chances. I would bring him back down to reality. This is what made our love work, made our relationship work, and what made this family superhero thing work.

I loved that my kids had their father in their life, and he was such an awesome father. I grew up without mine, he was never there. But I had a great stepfather who had been my dad since I was nine and had always been my children's grandfather. I told my mom about me drinking the elixir when I came home from school for the holiday break. She was so scared and confused, and she felt so bad about not being able to help me through this. For a while, she didn't like Saffore or Sylvester. She blamed them for my powers. But once she saw how well Sylvester protected me, and how much Saffore helped me with my powers, she softened. Once Sylvester and I became parents my mom supported us with the kids. Whenever I felt guilty about this superhero thing or being a mom she always told me,

"Hun, don't beat yourself up. Even though you may be intuitive and know almost everything about your kids, that won't make you perfect. No mother is perfect. But your kids still look at you like you are perfect. As long as you love them and care for them, you're perfect to them, and you can do no wrong. This superhero thing may get confusing, but God has blessed your family with these abilities. He'll guide you on how to use them. And since being a superhero is confusing, it helps the kids to know that they have a mom who cares for them, supports them, and knows exactly what they're going through."

My mom always knew exactly what to say, just like my husband. She always reminds me to be grateful that I had such amazing kids. A bulletproof sixteen-year-old Black son who was a nerd and an athlete. A beautiful 15-year-old daughter who was an amazing writer and cared so much for other people. Two funny twin boys who were sweet, creative, strong, lyrical, artistic, healing dancers who had each other's back. And a super sassy, super cute baby girl, who had the highest IQ of us all.

I arrived at headquarters now, dropped off by the driver who picked me up from the hotel and took me back every day. The chief thought it would be safer that way since I was by myself. The car also had a tracker on it so if anything goes wrong the chief, the CPD, and my family can see where I was. I appreciated their concern, but I could definitely take care of myself. Once inside headquarters, I went into the room where the meeting would take place. The chief was there.

"You ready?" the chief asked me.

"Yeah, I'm ready," I told him as I fixed my glasses and my wig.

"Okay, usually when the superintendent comes in, he sits at the head of the conference table. He'll be here, along with the mayor and a few other individuals. I'll introduce you. You'll be able to shake his hand. As you sit next to him, you'll be able to feel some things."

"So Chief, with you being a Black man, have you ever felt that he was racist?"

"Vivian, I'm a Black man, a police chief, and living in Chicago. I've met a lot of people who I felt were racist. And I'm not intuitive like you."

"I get what you're saying."

"He'll be coming in soon. He'll have some people with him. Maybe you'll see one of those guys who was a part of the monster." Just then, the door of the conference room opened, and the mayor walked in with the superintendent, a few assistants, and other administrative staff. They were having a conference with the alderman and some activists from North Lawndale about a recent shooting.

"This is my new assistant, Veronica. She just started working with me a few weeks ago," the chief introduced me to the superintendent.

"Good morning Veronica," he said as he held out his hand.

"Good morning, Superintendent," I shook his hand. He seemed a bit distant but when I shook his hand, I couldn't detect anything abnormal. No trembles down my spine, no hairs standing up on my arm, no chill bumps. Maybe something would happen once we had the conference.

"This is my new assistant, Ms. Ekoro. She just started working with me a few months ago," the superintendent said.

"Good morning, Veronica," Ms. Ekoro said.

"Good Morning," She was on the phone with one hand and holding some papers with the other, so she didn't hold out her hand for me to shake it.

I sat next to the superintendent. I still didn't feel anything. While we were talking to the alderman and activist, he didn't say anything. He seemed a bit aloof. Then the question came up, "What's going to happen to the cops who shot these children?" Everyone looked at the superintendent.

"We haven't decided yet," he said. After a few more questions, some negotiations, yelling, and, "Sirs, I assure you we're taking care of it," the conversation was over and nothing seemed to have been accomplished. The mayor and her people started to leave. Then the chief popped the question.

"Superintendent, I want to have a dinner party to celebrate your 30-year anniversary as superintendent in a couple of weeks. I would love it if you would approve?" the chief asked.

"I don't know, Chief. I have a lot to do…" the superintendent said.

"Come on. It'll be small and it will be at The Gwen Hotel with only a few guests."

"Okay, I'll be there," the superintendent said. Just then, Ms. Ekoro walked up to him and whispered something.

“We’ll be heading out, Chief. I’ll see you in a couple of weeks,” the superintendent said. They headed out the door of the conference room where the meeting took place.

“Did you pick up on anything?” the chief asked me.

“No, nothing,” I said.

“What about the assistant?”

“No, I didn’t get to shake her hand. But I have a feeling she’s connected to something. I’ll talk to Sylvester and the kids tonight and let them know. We haven’t encountered a woman who is a part of the monster, yet. So what are you all going to do about the two cops?”

“The superintendent told me the other day that we’ll give them a paid leave of absence,” the chief said.

“A paid leave?” I asked hysterically. “How can these guys get a paid leave for doing something so cruel?”

“I know. This is why I was hoping you would feel something or Ali would know something. I felt like the Superintendent wasn’t a part of the monster. But he has been making decisions that side with the crooked cops rather than disciplining them for their wrong doing." The chief said.

"Has he always done this?" I asked.

"No, it started around the time his wife died. A little bit after that, we had our first incident of a shooting of an unarmed Black man."

"How did his wife die?" I asked.

"She was shot by an armed Black teenager. The Black teen shot, her I guess, as revenge for the superintendent putting away his brother for some crimes he'd committed. When you all told me about this hatred monster, I thought maybe there was a connection. I could tell that some hatred developed in the superintendent's heart. After that, he just seemed complacent. We thought it was depression or anger. I mean, his wife died, it's understandable. But once you all told me that the monster mentioned him, I thought maybe, in some sort of way, the monster is connected to him. The superintendent never got any help or therapy after his wife died. And didn't really stop working."

"That's so horrible. But why would he release Haine and his members if he has some racial hatred in his heart?" I asked.

"Well, if I'm listening to you all correctly, the monster just represents hatred. Haine was connected to the monster you all defeated, the monster whose death stopped the gun violence in our Black and Brown neighborhoods. People have been turning their guns in and everything. But hatred is hatred. Bradley was able to figure out that this monster represented hatred against your own brother, your own breed. This hatred that the superintendent is feeling could be racist, but it's all hatred in the end. Haine spewed hatred, and what's going on with the cops now is also spewing hatred. And I'm sure with the gun violence going down, this is making the monster upset. I'm sure more will come along.

But to have a week in Chicago where there is no gun violence is wonderful."

"I see what you're saying," I said.

"This monster focused on Bradley's weak spot, losing Ahava and hating the killer. If it can do that to the Superintendent because of his wife, imagine what will go on in the CPD?"

"You're right. I'm going to go back to the hotel and call my family," I said.

"And make sure you stay close to the assistant at the dinner party, she may have a connection. And we want Ali to shake the superintendent's hand, but maybe there's some way she can shake the assistant's hand too," the chief said.

"Sounds good, Chief." I got in my truck and my driver drove back to the hotel. I called Sylvester and the kids once I was in my hotel room.

"Hi family!" I said once they pulled up my holographic image.

“Hey Ma!” they all said with smiles on their faces. I missed them so much.

“Hi Mommy!” Lena said excitedly.

“Hey baby, how you feelin’?” Sylvester asked me.

“I’m so much better now that I get to see you all!”

“So Mama, what happened with the superintendent? Did you crack the case?” Wil asked me.

“Nice cop talk, bro!” Cal told him.

“No, not yet. I actually shook the superintendent's hand today, and I didn’t feel anything.”

“That’s crazy, why would Kuzaliana say his name then?” Bradley asked.

“We’re still trying to understand. Now, the chief did give me some key information. He told me that around the time of the first shooting of an unarmed Black man, the superintendent’s wife died. She was shot and killed by an armed Black teenager who was seeking revenge. Since then, the superintendent has been letting the cops who shoot unarmed Black teenagers take a paid leave of absence. But that's not the facts they're reporting to the news outlets," I explained to my family.

"Wow, Ma, that's so messed up," Ali said.

"That's not all," I continued. "The superintendent has an assistant as well. I didn't get to shake her hand, but she told me her name. I wanted to see if Wil could tell me what it means."

"What's her name, Ma?" Wil asked.

"Her name is Ms. Ekoro," I told Wil.

"Let me see… That's Yoruba for crooked. I guess like a crooked cop," Wil said.

"That makes sense, then. It's her," Bradley said.

"Wait, we can't jump to conclusions until we get the facts. It doesn't have to be her, it could be someone connected to her as well," Sylvester said.

"Your father is right, kids. So in order to get close to her, the chief is going to host a dinner party at the hotel where I'm staying. This will be for the superintendent for his 30-year anniversary on the job. I'm going to go and I'm sure she'll be there too," I said.

"Oooooh Ma, can we come to the dinner party?" Cal asked.

"You guys can come, just in case something happens. You can sit outside of the hotel. But I want Ali to come with me to the part," I said.

"Why just Ali, Ma? We want to come too," Bradley asked.

"Because I want her to shake the superintendent's hand and tell me what he's feeling," I explained. "I'll also shake the assistant's hand to see if my intuition tells me anything. I'll ask her some questions to see if she's lying. I also want Ali to shake her hand to tell me what she feels."

"Okay Ma, so who am I supposed to be?" Ali asked me.

"We'll say that you're the chief's niece who's visiting him from out of town. You'll wear a wig and disguise like me as well. And we'll give you a different name. Act like you don't want to be there, but don't be super rude," I informed Ali.

"Got it!" Ali said.

"So Ma, why do you want us to come?" Cal asked.

"We don't want to make a scene at the Superintendent's dinner party. But just in case something happens, I want you all there. Also, maybe once the party is over we'll be able to follow his assistant. Find out where she's staying like we did with Arakunrin and Kuzaliana."

"Perfect plan, baby. We'll be ready," Sylvester said.

"Ali, you and I are going to go shopping for a disguise and dress you can wear. Lena, you can come too. It'll be great to have some mother-daughter time. And if you want Zoe to come as well, she can," I told Ali.

"Great, I'll be ready! I'm going to let Zoe know," Ali said.

"We'll go tomorrow morning. But tonight I'm going to have my driver take me back to headquarters," I said.

"What for, baby?" Sylvester asked me.

"I want to look inside their system, see if I can find any history on Ms. Ekoro."

I headed back to headquarters. Only security was there and many people were already gone. I tried checking the system. I was able to figure out how to work it in a matter of minutes, but there wasn't a lot of information on Ms. Ekoro. It stated that she had assisted a few Congressmen and a Supreme Court Judge, and it talked about her educational attainment. I decided to get in the truck and head back to the hotel. We were driving along and I was about to send a message to Sylvester and the kids when a car hit us and kept going. The car swerved, and we didn't see where it went. My driver asked me if I was okay.

“I’m fine, do you know what car hit us?” I asked my driver

“I don’t, it all happened so fast. I’ll text the chief and ask him to send another truck over.”

Just as he was contacting the chief, I called Sylvester to tell him what had happened. He asked me where I was. He was going to suit up, and he and Lena were going to come and get me. I heard five gunshots and looked out of the window and saw that my driver had been shot. Sylvester was calling my name from the phone. The shooter was opening up the car door. I stayed ducked down, but the person told me to get up and get out of the car. I got up and got out of the car with my hands up. They told me to face the car as they held a gun to my head.

“You and your family are getting yourselves into a lot of trouble,” they said, They were covered up, wearing all black.

“I don’t know what you’re talking about,” I responded afraid.

Just then, a forcefield appeared around me. I saw Sylvester and the kids — I guess Lena was able to get them there quickly. They knew my location because of the car's tracker. Bradley shot the person in the arm, and they started shooting back at my family, but everyone was inside the forcefield except for Sylvester and Bradley. Sylvester walked over to me and asked me if I was okay. Bradley was still shooting at the person as they got into their car and drove away. I couldn't see the car leaving. Sylvester told Lena to look at the car and license plate. She ran to it and saw the plate and car and ran back. Once the person was gone, Wil came out and healed my driver. He was still alive, so Wil just had to heal his wounds. After a while, the chief and some cops came with a new car. I told them what happened.

"Baby, you okay?" Sylvester asked.

"Mama, you okay? Are you hurt?" Wil asked as all of the kids walked up to look over me. I told them I was fine, and that they needed to get back to where they were staying. No one could hear them calling me Mama, I was undercover. I assured them that the chief would make sure I got back to the hotel.

"No, I don't want you back at that hotel. That person knew who you were, so you need to find somewhere else to stay," Sylvester said as he, the chief, the kids, and I stepped to the side to talk.

"She can stay at another hotel," the chief said. "Sylvester, I don't want you all to blow your cover. You all gotta go back to the apartment. We'll make sure she gets to another hotel safely."

"You okay, baby,? If you're not okay, we won't leave," Sylvester said.

"Baby, I'm fine," I told Sylvester. "I'll still take Lena and Ali with me tomorrow to go shopping. I'm okay, you all go to the apartment. I'll be fine. I'll call you when I get to my new hotel."

“Mommy, I saw the car and license plate,” Lena said once we all were done talking.

“What was it, baby?” I asked.

CHAPTER 2: NAOMI AND RUTH

After the accident and shooting, I was still a bit shaken up. When the person said that our family was in trouble, I became worried. Even though I knew we were safe, I didn't want anything to happen to the kids. I told Sylvester about it. He told me not to worry, that we'd find this monster and take it down and hopefully end the corruption inside the CPD once and for all. Lena told me about the car. It had a Washington D.C. license plate. I asked the chief if Ms. Ekoro had a D.C. license plate, but he told me she didn't. I still felt that she was connected to the monster. We still didn't know who the person was who hit the car, but hopefully we'd find out soon. I felt more comfortable being at this hotel. I felt that whoever was following us knew that I was undercover. I still wanted to take Lena and Ali shopping today. I was out of disguise, and Sylvester wanted to watch out for me and the girls. So as the girls and I shopped, he would keep the forcefield around the car while he and the boys were in it. Zoe was able to come with us. We went into Nordstrom first.

"I love that one!" Ali said as I tried on a dress. Zoe was next, and Lena just wanted to speed through and try on everything.

This was great! Spending time with my girls and seeing smiles on their faces was what I needed to make things better. I wanted to talk to Ali to see how she'd been feeling. It can be hard being an older girl with so many brothers and a little sister you have to take care of. I felt bad for leaving all of the kids, but especially her. It was like she had to be everyone's mom now that I was away.

"So how you feelin', hun?" I asked her.

"I'm okay, Mama. Uncle Saff is helping us figure out how to use our powers. The breathing and blocking technique is helping a lot. I've been writing a lot lately too," Ali said as she looked at dresses on some of the clothing racks.

"Oh yeah, about what?"

"Like you told us. Write about what we're feeling and doing as superheroes."

"And?"

"I don't know, I guess right now I just miss being home. I miss you and feel that everyone is so needy. And I'm trying to help Dad, but everyone needs you. I can't be you. There isn't much I can do for them. They want you. I miss Zoe, but I can't see her much. And I'm just trying to figure all of this out. It's been a crazy year for our family."

"Ali, do you want to stop doing this? If you ever want to stop, you can — or we can," I asked her.

"No, I love doing our family superhero thing. I just wish you could do this with us more. But I feel that soon we'll figure out who is connected to the superintendent. Then you'll be back with us."

"You sure?"

"Yeah Ma, I'm sure."

"I'm sorry, baby for giving you so much responsibility. We'll be done with this soon," I said as I hugged her.

"I think I like this dress," she said after we hugged. I'm sure she felt what I was feeling and wanted to make things better.

"Okay, try it on. See if you like it. Are you nervous about the dinner party?"

"No, I think we'll be okay," Ali answered me.

"Mommy, I found a dress!" Lena said.

"That's great, Lena, but you're not going to the dinner party. Remember?" I tried to explain to her.

"Okay! Can I still have the dress?"

“Okay!” I told her as I rolled my eyes and smiled. She was so cute.

“I’ll try this one on, Ma,” Ali said. Me and Ali were like Ruth and Naomi. We were always together, and wherever I went, she went. She was my girl, and I missed being with her. And I understood her missing being with me. I hoped we could find out who was connected to the hate monster when we had the dinner party.

“You love it?” I asked Ali as she stepped out of the dressing room. She looked beautiful.

“Yeah, I love it!” She told me.

“Me too!”

Today was the day for the dinner party. Ali had stayed with me the day before to get ready.

“So Mama, what if it is Ms. Ekoro? Do you think we’ll have to fight her at the hotel?”

“If we have to Ali, we have to. I’m hoping it is her.”

"Mama, the person who was trying to hurt you, was it a man or a woman?"

"It was a man, I could tell by the body. But it was a shorter man and not as muscular."

"Oh, I thought, if it was a woman, maybe it was her," Ali said.

"Yeah, but it doesn't mean it's not connected to her. I wonder why the license plate was from D.C.?"

"Yeah, same."

"Alright baby, it's almost time to be ready. Put this wig on," I told her. We got in the car with the guys and Lena. Sylvester drove us to the hotel where the dinner party was taking place. The chief was there already in one of the hotel party rooms. He asked me and Ali to stand by the door to greet guests. We shook a lot of hands, and Ali was able to find out a lot of secrets. A few more guests started to arrive.

"Senator, you and your wife look lovely this evening," I said.

“Mom, that wasn’t his wife,” Ali said as they walked away while she giggled.

“Stop laughing, girl,” I said. Then walked in the superintendent. I shook his hand, but I still didn’t get that funny feeling. Ali shook his hand.

“This is the chief’s niece. She’s visiting him from out of town,” I told the superintendent.

“Oh hi, young lady, nice to meet you. Sorry you had to be here tonight with all these old people,” the superintendent said to Ali.

“It’s okay, thank you!” Ali said.

“My assistant should be here in a bit. She may have another person with her,” the superintendent told us.

“Okay, thanks for letting us know,” I said.

“Mom, he was thinking about his wife,” Ali told me after the superintendent walked away. Wishing she was here. Was kind of sad. There is also anger, regret, and hatred for the guy who did it to her. The guy is behind bars, but he hates him. He was a young Black guy. You know, similar to who the cops have been killing lately here in Chicago. Maybe he hates anyone who reminds him of the man," Ali whispered.

"You know, you might be right." After a few more guests started to arrive, the superintendent's assistant came with her date.

"Hi Veronica!" I was finally able to shake her hand. I felt it. I felt what I was expecting to feel with the superintendent. Chills down my spine, hairs sticking up on my arm, chill bumps. I had to keep it together.

"Hi Ms. Ekoro, how are you? And who is this?" I asked

"This is my date Mr. Irira," Ms. Ekoro said. When I shook his hand, I got the same feeling.

"And who might this be?" she asked, talking about Ali.

"I'm the chief's niece, here from out of town," Ali said as she held out her hand for them to shake it.

"Oh, what is your name?" Ms. Ekoro said as she shook Ali's hand. Ali took a minute to answer her since she was shaking her hand.

"Kennedy, her name is Kennedy," I said. All I could think of was the expressway.

"Nice to meet you, Kennedy," Mr. Irira said as he shook her hand as well.

"Your seats are right this way," I told them.

"Ali, what's wrong?" I whispered to her after Ms. Ekoro and Mr. Irira walked away.

"Mom, it was freaky. I didn't see any memories like I have before when I held people's hands. I didn't really feel anything. Except strong hatred and crookedness. I've never felt hatred like that."

"So they are monsters. Text your brother and ask him what Irira means," I told Ali.

"I'm sure it means hatred, Ma. That's what I felt. But I'll ask him."

"Okay, baby."

"Mama?"

"Yeah, baby?"

"Was Mr. Irira the guy who was trying to shoot at you? You said he was small in stature, not a lot of muscle," Ali asked me.

"He does fit the description, but I don't know," I said.

"Wil got back to me, Ma. He said it means loathsome in Yoruba," Ali said.

Just then, Mr. Irira walked up and said,

"I left something in the car. I'll be right back."

"Are you parked far?" I asked.

"No, just in the hotel parking lot," he said as he ran out.

"Ali, tell your dad to pull into the hotel parking lot so he can see what car Mr. Irira drives. Tell him how he looks."

Ali texted her dad using the bracelet Saffore had created for us. Sylvester pulled into the parking lot. He saw Mr. Irira.

However, he didn't see them because Sylvester had the forcefield around the car.

"Okay Mama, he got back to me. He said he's in a Black Lincoln," Ali said.

"Ask him to check the license plate and ask Lena if she remembers the car and the license plate number." We were doing this while everyone was mixing and mingling. The chief looked at me to see what was going on. I winked at him to let him know we thought we found something.

"Mama, he said the license plate says D.C., and Lena said that she remembers this license plate. It's from the car that drove away the day we came to help you."

"So it is him," I said.

"Mama, what is he doing here in a car from D.C.?"

"I don't know, baby. That means he knows that we're here and who I am."

"Dad is going crazy, he keeps saying he wants to hurt this guy. I'm sorry, this monster," Ali told me.

"Tell your father to calm down. Ask him what the man got from the car."

"He said he can't see. The windows are tinted. And he said he's coming back from the parking lot. He should be entering the building soon. Dad also said they're following him and they're going to sit right across the street to watch everything."

"Okay baby, good job." I walked over to the chief and tapped him on the shoulder to tell him that we should get started with dinner as Mr. Irira walked back in.

"Let's sit down for dinner, everyone," the chief announced. We were strategic in placing Ms. Ekoro across from me along with her guest. Mixing and mingling was going on at the dinner table. So I started asking questions, wanting to see if he would tell me anything.

"So how did you two meet?" I asked them.

"Oh, we met a long time ago in D.C.," Ms. Ekoro said.

"Oh, what was going on in D.C.?" I asked.

“I was an assistant for someone who worked there, in politics. It’s a lot easier being the assistant for the Superintendent of Police in Chicago,” she said.

“We’re in a long distance relationship. I still work there,” Mr. Irira said.

“Oh, what do you do?” I asked.

“I’m a vice presidential assistant. Well, one of them,” he said to me, looking hostile.

“Oh, fancy! How long have you had this position?” I asked.

“Quite some time now. I just can’t seem to let it go,” he said

“So you just came here to go to the superintendent’s party? That seems like a tough job to get away from. Especially for something so menial,” I said as he had his head down to take a slurp of his soup.

“I figured Ms. Ekoro needed me. A couple of our family members died in a house fire. So I figured she needed me for comfort and backup,” Mr. Irira said.

“How tragic. And did you say *our* family members?” I pried.

“Yeah.” He responded, dropping his spoon in his soup, putting his head up, and wiping his mouth. I hadn’t touched my food.

“I thought you said you all were dating?” I said as I looked him in the eye.

He just smirked. He leaned forward a little bit and whispered,

“This is a fight you don’t want. You and your family won’t win. We’re everywhere. And we’ll have someone in Chicago again sooner than you think.”

“This fight may be bigger than my family and I, but we’re more prepared than you think. We’ll continue to fight against you and the hatred you bring. We won't stop until you all are gone. You know why?" I asserted.

"Why?" He asked.

"Because we're splendid!" Just as I said this, he shot me in the leg. I fell out of my chair. Ali came down by me. He started to shoot at the chief as the chief held up his gun to shoot at him. He shot the chief in the arm. Many people were screaming, running, ducking, crouching, exiting, trying to get out of the hotel. Ms. Ekoro and Mr. Irira started to head for the door, shooting and telling people to get out of the way. Many of the officers who were there tried shooting them as well, but to no avail. They got out of the hotel party room and were trying to flee. All I remember is Ali calling me, but everything looked fuzzy.

"MAMA GET UP!" Ali said to me.

"I'm okay, baby, call your father and tell him we need them."

CHAPTER 3 - MOTHER LION

Many people had stormed out of the building, but some were still crouching down, hiding in the party room, and more officers had come in. There were also police officers surrounding the hotel. Sylvester and the kids came into the building. Wilson healed me, the chief, and some other people. Little did I know my family had entered the hotel when Mr. Irira did. No one saw them because they had used the forcefield to get in. They were standing right in the lobby and we were on the 5th floor. When they heard the gunshots, Lena rushed them up the stairs. I had only seen Wilson, Sylvester, and Lena.

"Dad, where are Bradley and Cal?" Ali asked.

"They're in the hotel lobby waiting for the monsters to get downstairs. Suit up and square up, we have to join them in the lobby. Chief, tell everyone to get out of the hotel."

"Got it!" The chief had officers standing around the entire time. He had told them that something might happen tonight. He ordered them to get everyone out of the hotel as quickly as they can.

"What's going on?" the superintendent asked the chief.

"We're trying to catch your assistant, we think she's not who she says she is," the chief responded. The superintendent looked confused as the chief helped him to get out of the hotel.

Ali and I ran to the stairs where Sylvester, Wilson, and Lena were. While we headed out, we suited up and Lena got all of us downstairs to the lobby with Calhoun and Bradley. The two monsters headed to the lobby in their human form, but not using the stairs. They used the elevator. Once in the lobby, they started shooting. Bradley stood in front of the door, and the bullet hit him. He absorbed it.

"Did you really think that would work?" Bradley said sarcastically.

Calhoun picked up the receptionist table and hit the two monsters with it. By this time, we had come downstairs. Ali, Wilson, the chief, and I tried to get as many people out as possible. Mr. Irira and Ms. Ekoro started to change into the monster.

"Dad, what's the plan?" Cal asked as they were changing.

"Is everyone out of the hotel?" Sylvester asked.

"I don't think so, Pops," Bradley said.

"I was thinking maybe get everyone out and have Samson tear the walls down," Sylvester said.

"Can't do that, there are too many people here," Ali said.

"What if we led him out into the city?" Sylvester said.

“Baby, that’s way too many people. We’re on Michigan Avenue,” I said.

“Right, Dad, we can’t mess up the Magnificent Mile,” Ali said.

“We gotta lead it out because we gotta burn it down. That’s the only way to get rid of it so we can stop this hatred,” Sylvester said.

“Alright,” I said.

“Alright, Bradley, start shooting at it. Make it mad. Cal, throw that table at it.”

We started to head out into the streets. We told the chief the plan, so he had some of the cops stop the traffic so we could get by easily. We headed off to the Magnificent Mile from the Gwen Hotel then to the Chicago Lake Shore. Even though it seemed like a long time, it only took about 10 minutes. There were people screaming, running, and stopping in their tracks to observe everything. The monster that was now a dark blue, with gold horns, and shimmering gold flecks on its body followed us. He didn't come through the door. He broke a piece of the hotel and made a bigger opening for himself. We got through the traffic, blocking his hits and swings as we headed towards Lake Shore Drive. Once on the Lake Shore, we started to fight it. It was strong. Stronger than the monsters we'd fought previously. Sylvester would make us disappear so it couldn't see us. Lena threw some sand in its eyes so it couldn't see. Cal pushed it down, and Lena ran around it to create a fire to burn it. It caught on fire, starting to scream as it burned.

Before it died it said,

"You'll never be able to stop the hatred." Then it disintegrated. As we stood over it, we wondered what would happen now that the monster was gone. We still had to talk to the chief and the superintendent and explain everything.

"We did it!" Cal said to Wil as they high-fived.

"I have a feeling this isn't it. I know that's your line, baby!" Sylvester said.

"You're right, it's not. The man that you all saw, Mr. Irira, he works in D.C. He's a presidential assistant. There are others in D.C.," I said.

"Well baby, I'm sure there are others around the world. What are we supposed to do about it? Our job is to protect Chicago," Sylvester said.

"I know but, maybe if we could get the monsters in D.C., we wouldn't need to protect Chicago. The hatred would stop. We'd be defeating the monster in the highest office in America," I said.

"Won't do any good, Ma, more would come," Bradley said.

"Well then let them come, but at least we defeated what's already here. Mr. Irira told me that he came because Ms. Ekoro needed backup. Because of us, and because of us defeating Arakunrin and Kuzaliana, he knew she wouldn't be able to fight us on her own. We defeated this monster, so we have to try and defeat other monsters. Who else will?" I explained.

"But Ma, how are we going to get all the way to D.C.?" Ali asked me.

"Maybe the chief can help," I said.

"Mommy, I found this at the hotel," Lena said to me, giving me a phone. "It fell out of the man's pocket, Mr. Irira. It has the symbol on it that's been on all of the other monsters. I saw it, so I picked it up."

"This must be a way that they communicate," Wil said.

"Wait, you mean to tell me that they're a monster that has been around for centuries and they need a phone to communicate? Man, that's so 2000 and late. We at least have bracelets," Cal said.

"But they have to blend in with everyone else. Everyone uses a phone, so they need a phone," Ali said.

"We can use it. See who we can talk to and what we can find," Sylvester said. Afterwards, we headed back to the hotel. The chief and the superintendent were standing outside.

“What did you all do to my assistant?” the superintendent asked us.

“Superintendent, she wasn’t who you thought she was. We think she’s been a part of why so many cops have been killing so many unarmed Black teenagers,” the chief explained.

“What are you all talking about?” the superintendent asked.

“Superintendent, I know that you’re still mourning the loss of your wife. But I think you’ve also developed some hatred in your heart towards the person who killed her,” the chief stated.

“Chief, that's none of your business. And if you want to keep your job, you had better keep your mouth shut,” the superintendent asserted.

"Superintendent, I think you need to get some help. Some therapy or counseling to help you deal with the death of your wife," the chief told him calmly.

"I said…" the superintendent started.

"Superintendent, I had a best friend who was shot and killed during a school shooting by someone who hated people of all races. You see, Superintendent, my superpower is to absorb and shoot bullets. But I couldn't protect someone I cared about. I wasn't there to protect my best friend, and he died. I know you must feel the same way. You're probably upset with yourself for not being there for your wife. So you hated anyone who reminded you of the person who did this to your wife. But it's not your fault, and it's not that person's fault. It's hatred. Hatred makes people feel this way. I'm sorry, but what the chief is saying is true. It helps to talk to someone about it," Bradley told the chief.

The superintendent started to cry, and Bradley began to hug him. I was so proud of him for helping the superintendent and helping him to know that he understood.

"Splendid Saba, thank you for all your help. Go home. You guys deserve some rest!" the chief told us, and we did just that. But we knew that our work didn't stop there.

We stayed home for a couple of days. I was happy to finally be home with the kids and my husband again. The chief informed us that the superintendent was getting some help, and things were changing inside the CPD. We hadn't heard anything about anymore school shootings, no more gang and gun violence, and no more shooting of unarmed Black children and adults in Chicago. The news showed the fight that we had with the monster, and all news outlets were talking about it. But there were still things happening across America. As we all were sitting on the couch in our living room watching the news a phone rang.

Ring. Ring. Ring.

“That’s not the superhero line,” Sylvester said.

“Pops, it’s the phone that we picked up from the monster,” Bradley said.

“Answer it Bradley. Put it on speaker.” Sylvester said.

“Hello,” Bradley said.

“Hello, Splendid Saba,” a voice said from the other end of a private call.

“Who is this?” Sylvester said. We were all sitting on the sofa surrounding my husband.

“You know who this is. You’ve been annihilating my brothers and sisters all summer,” the voice on the other end continued. “Let me tell you. You don’t know what you’re dealing with. This nation was built on hatred, crookedness, killing, and racial hatred. You’ll never be able to stop us. But I would love to take you all down. Especially since you’ve defeated some of the greatest members of my crew. I want my revenge, and I’ll plaster you all across America to show that we're nothing to mess with. You wanna get to D.C. to battle me? The phone call will be coming soon, so we can end the Splendid Saba once and for all," just then, the voice on the other end hung up the phone.

"Hello? HELLO?" Sylvester said.

"So who could this be?" Ali asked.

"They know us, but we don't know them?" Cal asked.

Ring. Ring. Ring.

This time the ring came from the superhero line.

"Hello?" Sylvester said.

"Hey Sly, this is the Chief. You were saying something about D.C., right?"

"Yeah, what's up?" Sylvester asked.

"The mayor got a call from the White House," the chief said. "Then she called me about it to see if I knew how to get in touch with you all. I told her I might. The president wants you all to come to D.C., to the White House. The president wants to honor you and your family during the Medal of

Freedom Ceremony for the great work you're doing as superheroes in Chicago."

PART 6: BULLETPROOF BLACK BOY

CHAPTER 1: INVINCIBLE

Invincible. Sometimes I struggled with the meaning of that word. I don't think anyone is truly invincible, not even me. Weapons didn't hurt me. I could absorb and shoot bullets — throw anything my way, and my body didn't break. But that was just the outside of me. The inside of me was not invincible. My mind was easily penetrated. I was more sensitive than I would have liked to be. If I couldn't get hurt, how would I die? I'd never told anyone my feelings about this. I was always thinking about how I'd die. Would it be poison? Would it be old age? Would it be my health? Would I outlive my entire family? Ever since Ahava's death, I'd been consumed with the idea of death and how I'd die. I always wondered what Ahava felt before he died. What did he see? What did he think? Did he suffer? Did he die helping someone else? Did he die trying to get out of the school? Did he die wishing I was there? Did he die wishing I could save him? Did he die angry at me for not being there? I knew everyone told me not to blame myself or not to feel bad for not being there. But how could I not feel bad? How could I not feel bad for being a bulletproof Black guy? Because of my abilities, I always felt like I was supposed to save everyone. Because of what happened with Ahava, I always felt that saving others made up for not saving him.

"Everybody all packed? We'll be heading to Uncle Saff's soon to head for D.C.," Pops told us.

"Bradley, while we're in D.C., make sure to keep that hoodie off," he said to me.

Ever since what happened to Trayvon Martin, my pops has hated hoodies. I was only five years old when this happened, and my little brothers were only two. But for some reason, he took the whole Black boy in a hoodie thing to another level. Didn't he realize that I was bulletproof? That it wasn't the hoodie that killed Trayvon Martin? I guess no matter how bulletproof your Black son is, you still worry. So when he told me to take my hoodie off, I just did it. My dad may have been a bit overprotective when it came to me. I mean, I'd be eighteen in a couple of years. But I understand his fear. It must not have been easy, raising three Black sons. And to top it off, even though I was bulletproof, I was basically a weapon. When I found out that I was a weapon, it scared me. I mean, people fear Black guys already. Now I could shoot bullets. So did that mean people would fear me in my superhero form? If anyone ever figured out my identity, would they hurt me? Maybe that's why Mom and Dad are always so worried.

"Alright y'all, before we leave I want us to discuss something important," my pops told us, and we all sat on the couch. "What we're about to face is something bigger than what we've ever faced before. Yes, we defeated racial hatred in Chicago. Yes, we ended gang and gun violence in Chicago. And yes, we ended police brutality in Chicago. But we may find something bigger than all of this when we go to D.C. This monster is out for vengeance. We thought the hatred we fought was strong, but this hatred runs deeper. This hatred wants us dead. We may have to fight against it before we step foot in D.C. We may encounter obstacles on our plane ride to our nation's capital. You all are strong, you've been practicing, and you have to make sure you're ready for whatever comes our way."

"Dad, do you think we'll have to fight Chuki and Taifa?" Cal asked.

I was hoping we would. Just like they wanted their vengeance, I wanted mine.

"We might, but they're not as strong. I believe that the monster we need to fight is much stronger. Saff will be coming with us because we'll need his expertise. And we may have to protect him because he's not used to this. Don't be afraid. We are strong, and as long as we stay focused on helping each other, we'll get the job done," my pops explained.

"Daddy, do you think that if Chuki and Taifa are there, they'll go for Bradley?" Ali asked as she looked at me.

"Why do you think they'll come for me? They want us all gone," I asked looking back at her confused.

"Bradley, don't you see? They came for you in the beginning — they wanted you, not us. They believed that you could be a weapon, they wanted to weaponize you. They wanted to use a bulletproof Black boy to shoot bullets and kill White supremacists. They wanted to start a race war with you. Possibly the ultimate hatred in America. So they'll probably come for you," Ali said, looking worried.

"But we won't let anything happen to Bradley. And Bradley you can't be concerned with getting revenge because of Ahava's death. And you can't seek revenge for them shooting me. This fight is not just for you, and it's not just about you. It's to end hatred in America," my mom said.

"Well, son, are you ready? Can you handle this?" my pops asked me, and I just stood there for a while.

I didn't know for sure if I was ready. If I could handle this. But I just responded,

"Yeah pops, I was born ready."

"Alright, this is what you were made for. This is what we all were made for. This will be splendid," my pops said to us.

"So Dad, are we taking a regular plane?" Wil asked.

"No, Saffore has his pilot's license and a private jet, so we'll be taking that," my pops responded. Everyone paused with their suitcases as we were headed out the door.

"What?" my pops said as he turned around to look at us.

"Daddy, Uncle Saff is a pilot with a private jet, and we're just now hearing about it?" Ali asked.

“Wait a minute Dad, how much money does Uncle Saff have?” Cal asked.

“Kids, your uncle is rich. Now let's go,” my mom said.

We were now on Uncle Saff’s private jet. He was actually a great pilot. My dad put a forcefield around it so no one could see us in the air. My mom showed us that all of the news outlets were talking about our family. Everyone was showing images of how we fought the monster downtown and ended police brutality and gang and gun violence in Chicago. Now we were headed to D.C. to receive the Presidential Medals of Freedom. I never would’ve thought my family would make such a big difference in Chicago, let alone receive a medal of freedom for it. After hearing all of the praises, we knew the negative comments were coming soon. My little brothers read some of the comments on YouTube. Many of the comments were positive, but then the haters came.

"So America has Black superheroes? A Black superhero family?"

"They must be robots."

"Why are we honoring a Black superhero family?"

"Why are they Black?"

"I don't care that they are superheroes, I don't want them saving me."

"First BLM, now this."

"They don't represent true American superheroes. They're not my superheroes."

On that last comment my pops said,

"Cal and Wil, don't worry about what people think. Remember our fight is bigger than this. And hopefully we can defeat this monster to stop all of these comments from hurting others."

"Always remember that people talked about Jesus too. So whatever anyone has to say about you isn't as big of a deal," my mama said.

“Gotta be greater than the haters,” Wil and Cal said at the same time.

Sometimes I did wonder — why did God choose a Black family to give these powers to? Why did he choose a Black superhero family to fight gang and gun violence in Chicago? Why us? Why did Cal have sickle cell *and* super strength? Why was I a bulletproof sixteen-year-old Black boy? Why was Wil a healer and linguistic? Why was Mama intuitive? Why could our dad mimic our powers and make force fields? Why could Ali feel what others felt? And why did Lena have an eidetic memory and the ability to move faster than the speed of light? What did it all mean? My parents had always said that God has a plan, and to everything there is a season, and a time to every purpose.

“You okay, B?” Ali asked me as she sat down next to me. I guess I had that daydreaming look on my face.

“Yeah A, I’m good!” I told her with my head down. She just kinda looked at me.

"Now I can hold your hand and understand how you feel, or you can just tell me," she said, smirking.

"Okay, why us? Why were we chosen? And why are we a Black family of superheroes?" I asked her

"You still don't know?" Ali asked me.

"And you do?" I asked her.

"Bradley, who better to fight against racial hatred in America than a Black family? Who would care more about ending gang and gun violence and police brutality — not only in Chicago, but in America — than a Black family? Also, we give many people hope."

"You got a point. So why do we have the powers we have?"

"You say that like it's a hard question."

"Well then, tell me," I told Ali.

"Our powers represent the struggles that our people have faced. Struggles that everyone faces. And what's needed in this world. We'll start with Dad. Black men are not seen as protectors. Black dads are not seen as protectors, and they are not seen as present. We have a Black dad who is a present and who is a protector, and with his power to create force fields, he protects any and everybody. He can mimic our powers because he is the head of our home, and we come from him. Mama is intuitive and can figure out any system. She represents the Black mother who is portrayed as strong but not always portrayed as maternal. She is intuitive like all mothers can be, but it goes further than that. And she can figure out any system because she represents the intellect of Black women that is not always acknowledged. Cal has sickle cell, something that usually impacts Black people, but he is strong regardless. He represents our people being strong regardless of their pain. And their strength to overcome the many obstacles we've faced and continue to face. Wil is gentle, showing that Black boys and Black men are not the monsters that they're painted to be. He's a healer, which is what the world needs. But our people in particular never received healing for what happened to them during slavery. Not to mention, they are the most negatively affected by the medical field. And he can speak every language because it represents the communication and connectedness of all people. Something that's lacking globally, but especially in America. Something that is needed to stop hatred. Lena has super speed, which I think is just because she's so little and hyper. But she has an eidetic memory and a high IQ, which represents our people being seen as inferior when it comes to academics, even though we've always been intelligent. And you being an invincible, bulletproof, Black boy represents all of the innocent Black people who have died in this country, especially young males and young children, due to gun violence. And even though you have an infinite number of bullets, you still don't want to hurt anyone."

"When did you figure all this out?" I said as I laughed a bit at my sister's wisdom.

"I read too, bro, I don't just write. And I know our family was chosen for a reason. We as humans don't always know why God does the things he does, and we may never know. But he chooses who he chooses for a reason. Everyone we read about in the Bible was chosen for a purpose, and that main purpose was for Jesus to get here and die for us. I don't know everything that our family will do, but us doing this makes sense."

"And what about you? Why do you have the ability you have?"

"I represent empathy and care for one another. Being able to feel another person's pain helps you to understand them. If there was more empathy, there would be less hatred."

"Thanks A!" I said as I hugged her. Anytime I felt confused, let down, or just didn't know what direction I should take, Ali could always talk some sense into me and clear my mind.

“Of course B! You ready to have your enemies stand before you?” she asked me, I didn’t know how I felt about that.

“I guess. Y’all will be there, so I know we can handle it.”

“Guys, we’re almost there,” Uncle Saff said as he walked to us all from the cockpit.

“Uncle Saff, why aren’t you still driving the jet?” Lena asked.

“I was never driving it, niecy wiecy. I only sat up there to make y’all feel comfortable. Just like there are cars that can drive without humans, I have a jet that can soar without humans.”

“So Unc, we didn’t know you were rich,” Wil said.

“Exactly how do you make your money?” Cal asked.

“Isn’t it obvious? I’m a scientist, therapist, and inventor. I don’t just invent gadgets for y’all, or therapize y’all, I do a lot of stuff. I have a high IQ like Lena, but not as high as hers."

"So Uncle Saff, did you create another elixir and give it to other humans?" Ali asked.

"No, I think the Splendid Saba is enough. And that's why no one should ever know how you got your powers. So just say you were born with them whenever someone asks. If our world ever needs more superheroes, I still have the elixir formula locked away in a safe place where no one would ever find it," Uncle Saff responded.

"Where is it?" Lena asked.

"No one needs to know. We'll only use it when our world needs more heroes," Uncle Saff explained.

"But they have us, why would they need more?" Cal asked.

"Y'all can't be everywhere at once. So there may be other people that need powers. And if God directs me to them, just like He directed Samuel to David, I'll give them the elixir," Uncle Saff said.

"Hey y'all look out the window! Welcome to D.C.!" my pops said to us.

Uncle Saff landed the jet. Well, it landed itself on his D.C. property. Who knew that he had a place in D.C.? It was much better than staying at that small apartment of my dad's friend. Of course, Saff had a smaller lab here that we could go to as well. Downstairs, there was an underground space with no windows and one entrance and exit. Except inside the house. He wanted to perform some more experiments on us and make our powers stronger.

"So do y'all think you'll be able to burn this hatred monster like you have before?" Uncle Saffore asked.

"We don't know. I don't think that'll work here with this monster. I was shocked it worked with the other monsters.

It'll be stronger than before, and it'll be expecting this tactic," my mama said.

"So what's the plan?" Cal asked.

"For the first time, I don't know what the plan is," my pops said. We all looked confused.

"Uncle Saffore, is there any power that one of us has that may help to defeat this monster?" Ali asked.

"I don't know. If you all are fighting against hatred, this may be the strongest hatred monster you've ever had to battle. I don't know what would defeat it. Like your mom said, we didn't know fire would defeat the others. And knowing that fire defeated the others, I'm sure they'll be expecting this tactic," Uncle Saff responded.

"So what should we do?" Cal asked, and we all got quiet. Then I had an idea.

"What if we fight the monster the same way we've fought all the other ones?" I said.

"Bradley, we just said that wouldn't work, weren't you here?" Ali said.

"Right bro, stay with us," Cal said.

"No, hear me out. We'll start off fighting how we usually do and give them what they expect," I said.

"Okay, still not hearing anything different," Wil said.

"Then we fight them collectively," I said.

"Bradley, we always fight together," my mama said.

"Right, but the monster gets stronger once it combines. What if we combine all of our powers?" I asked.

"Bradley, we can't come together physically, we're human," Wil said.

"That's not what I'm saying. Uncle Saff, is there a way that our powers can get stronger if we're more connected? Like if we all held hands, or synced our bracelets, or something like that?" I asked.

"That might be a plan, Bradley. I don't know if it could work. I don't have all of my equipment that I have in

Chicago, but we can try. So what are you thinking, nephew? That if y'all combine it'll be a new superpower?" Uncle Saff asked.

"I don't know Unc, maybe?" I said.

"Alright then, let's find out. Y'all step into the chamber." We all got in like Uncle Saff said. He got on his machine and started doing some tests. I'd never seen my Uncle work so fast. He had a determined look over his face. He looked like a mad scientist. His eyes were down, his back was hunched, he kept rubbing his hand, his nostrils were flared.

"Bradley, what made you think of this?" my pops asked while we all were in the chamber.

"Well Pops, I thought that hatred would end in America if more people were united. So since we're here to fight a hatred monster, we need to be united. I got the idea from Ali," I had to give my sister her props.

"Awww, you were listening?" Ali was so happy.

“Yeah, I guess that’s part of us being a family as well. Our powers don’t just work together in a fight. We gain knowledge, wisdom, and clarity from each other,” I said.

“Good idea, kids!” my mama said as she hugged us.

“Alright y’all, let’s try the bracelets.” So we did what Uncle Saff said. We put our bracelets together, but nothing happened.

“Uncle Saff, why didn’t anything happen?” Lena asked.

“I think it’s because y’all’s superpowers aren’t found in your bracelets. They’re found in you. We’re going to have to try something different,” Uncle Saff said.

CHAPTER 2: FAMILY STRENGTH

"Alright everyone, suit up. The ride is here for us to head to the White House," my dad yelled to all of us.

We pressed our bracelets and suited up before we headed out. There were a lot of people surrounding the White House once we got there. Some of them were holding up signs that showed how much they loved us. It was cool to see that we had impacted so many people. Inside the White House, the tour guide gave us all of the information we needed to pass an American history exam. We walked around more and more. As we got close to the Oval Office, Mom said that she was getting that feeling. That feeling where the hair on her arms stood up. Where she got tingles down her spine. Where she got chill bumps. We headed into the Oval Office. The president and vice presidents were there with many photographers, newscasters, and assistants.

“Good morning Splendid Saba! Welcome to Washington D.C., our nation's capital,” the president said. He shook all of our hands. No one felt weird after shaking his hand, so he wasn’t a part of the monster.

“Good Morning Mr. President, Vice President.” My pops started out. “Thank you for inviting us and honoring us with this medal.”

“With all the work that you’ve done in Chicago, of course. We never would’ve thought that you would end police brutality and gang and gun violence in Chicago,” the vice president said.

“You’ll have to excuse us, Mr. President. Our family is a bit shocked about receiving such an honor. We didn’t know that you would know about the work we’re doing in Chicago,” my mama said.

"Oh, I didn't. My presidential assistants told me. And one of the vice presidential assistants told the vice president. Recently one of the vice presidential assistants went to Chicago. I'm guessing they died during the chaos with the monster that you all defeated. We'll be having a ceremony in honor of their death soon. Anyway, once they told us about it, I called the mayor in Chicago and told them that I needed to give you all a medal of freedom. It was all our assistants' idea," the president explained.

The President turned towards his assistants so they could come forward. They walked forward, all three of them together, and I recognized two of them. And I'm guessing the one I didn't recognize was their leader. They introduced themselves one by one, held their hands out, and said,

"Good morning Splendid Saba. I'm Chuki." It was him. He looked a bit different, but had the same eyes.

"Good morning, I'm Taifa." It was him. He looked different as well, but had the same voice and eyes.

“Welcome! Glad you could make it. I’m Tarehe.”

This was the guy in the middle, who I believed to be their leader. My dad shook their hands first. Then my mom, and she seemed to be frozen. Then me, they squeezed my hand and said hello to me specifically. Then Ali, who seemed to be shaken with fear. Then the twins. Then Lena, who didn’t hold out her hand to shake their hand back.

“Well, shall we get started with the ceremony?” the vice president said.

We stood one by one, accepting our medals. They were placed around us. Then, in front of all the cameras and newsfeeds, the president asked my dad,

“So I should ask the question we all want to know. How did you all get your powers? Are you from a different planet or something like that?”

My pops responded, “No, nothing like that, Mr. President. We were born with them. They're blessings from God!”

"Well we are blessed to have you all!" Everyone clapped their hands after the president said this.

The president and vice president thanked us again for coming. The photographers and newscasters were escorted out. The presidents talked to us for a bit and after everyone left Chuki whispered something in the president's ear.

"I don't mean to be rude, but I have some more important business to take care of. Our assistants would like to escort you out," the president said as security escorted him out. Taifa whispered something, and then we went out into the hallway. The hallway was clear. Tarehe, Taifa, and Chuki turned towards us and we faced them. It looked like a standoff in an old western movie.

"So Wil, what does Tarehe mean?" I whispered to Wil.

"For some reason, I don't know," Wil responded and I looked at him, confused.

"Whatchu mean you don't know?" I asked.

Just then, when I asked Wil that, Chuki shot me in the leg, and I fell down. For the first time in my life, I had felt a bullet and began to bleed. It was like a shock went through my body. For a moment, I wasn't present as I looked at the blood on my hand. I began to fall, and all of my senses went away. My mama didn't see it coming. All I remember was seeing Wil's face when he got down by me and tried to heal me, but he couldn't. Cal ran and tried punching Chuki in the face, but his strength seemed to disappear. He started to have a sickle cell crisis, pain washing over him. At this point, he was just a regular thirteen-year-old boy. Chuki picked him up by the collar and threw him. Lena tried to move fast and couldn't. My dad came to my side and mom came to Cal's side. Ali bent down by me and my dad and looked around, confused. Chuki held a gun to my dad's head. Taifa held a gun to my mom's head.

Tarehe stood there and said,

"Well isn't this splendid?" He laughed, "I have you all right where I want you. I should kill you now, but first, allow me to introduce myself. I know that you all have the power to speak different languages. Well, not now. My name is history. Together we represent historical hatred in this nation. And I thought we would never be defeated until you all came along. You and your family had me scared for a while there. You really put up a fight. Defeating some of my best members. But then, we knew we had to bind the strong man, or the strong family I guess. We said we were going to get rid of you once and for all…"

"Where are our powers?" Lena asked.

"Little girl, didn't your parents teach you that it's rude to interrupt?" Tarehe asked.

"Lena, baby come by me. Don't say anything," my mama said.

"Bradley, I wanted you to know what it feels like to feel pain for the first time. Isn't it agonizing? Let me tell you why we came to you, Bradley Benjamin Stanton. We wanted you. We saw how low you were, and we saw that hatred would develop in your heart. Imagine how people across America would hate each other when they saw a teenage Black boy use his ability to shoot and absorb bullets to shoot some White supremacists. Then we could use you in wars and have you create hatred everywhere. This was the plan. We could have created so much hatred with you. But your family had to come save you. They figured out where we were. And that was our fault; we underestimated you all. But not today. We know that you all are strong and can't be defeated. So we knew we had to take your powers away. You'll never be able to erase the hatred. This country was built on hatred. This nation operates on hatred. And don't worry Bradley. We'll still use you for our cause, right after we kill your family."

"NO!" I said. Before they shot, and while Tarehe was talking, Ali looked at her bracelet that Saffore made and the message he'd sent.

Take off the medals.

Saffore had placed cameras inside of our masks to see everything that we saw. He also placed sensors in our bracelets to know our blood pressure, weight, fatigue levels, and if anything was different. He noticed that once the medals were placed on us, they took our powers away. Ali ripped off my pop's medal right when Tarehe ended his speech. Our medals were laced with VX, a nerve agent that caused our powers to stop just like it causes a regular human's nerves to stop. Because Saff had made our suits resistant to anything, the VX didn't penetrate the suit into our skin, even though it did stop our powers. The president hadn't touched the medal, only the fabric so nothing had happened to him. I guess we now knew what could make us normal. For some reason, it didn't feel right, being normal. I had always imagined what it might feel like, it was…vulnerable. After Ali ripped my pops' medal off, he used Lena's super speed, removing the guns and all of our medals. He healed me and Cal using Wil's powers. He crushed the guns using Cal's powers and placed a forcefield around our family. All of the medals were in Chuki's hand when he looked up again.

Then, to Chuki, Taifa, and Tarehe's surprise, we were all standing up in front of them. Then my pops removed the forcefield and said,

"Family, be splendid!"

After working with Saffore, our powers and fighting skills had improved. Cal hit Chuki in the face like he wanted to do before. This sent him flying into the Oval Office. I took on Tarehe, starting to shoot at him. Lena started to shock Taifa since she was moving so fast. Of course, this made them upset and they started to combine.

"That's how it's done!" Lena said.

Then I told everyone to head outside on the lawn of the White House. I never thought that my family would be fighting our nation's historical hatred on the front lawn of the

White House. Many people were standing around to watch. We saw smoke come out of the top of the White House. This monster was different from the ones we've fought before. It was bigger and stronger, and all of the images that represent hatred in America appeared on its body. These historical hatred images were things we did know about and many things that we didn't know about. Things that have been buried within history. For a moment, we stood there in awe of the images we saw. Many of the people who were standing around watching were now gone. The monster had scared them away. It was still trying to get out of the White house to come towards us. As it sped towards us we tried to combine our powers.

"Are you all ready?" my mama asked us.

"B, are you sure this is going to work? We haven't worked out all the kinks," Cal asked.

"We have to try, or we'll never know," I said.

"Wait, what if one of us gets hurt by doing this? Or what if one of us dies doing this?" Wil said.

"Well if we don't try, a lot of people will die. We will be okay, don't worry," my pops said. "Grab each other's hands, be strong, and remember: be splendid."

My pops created a forcefield around everyone else to make sure we don't hurt anyone except the monster. The monster was still running on the White House lawn. I held Cal's hand, Cal held Wil's hand, Wil held Ali's hand, Ali held Lena's hand, Lena held Mama's hand, and Mama held Pops' hand. We told each other we loved each other because we didn't know what was going to happen.

As my pops was about to take my hand, he said,

"Great job, Son. Not only did you find a way to save us, you found a way to save America. I love you, Son!."

"I love you too, Pops." He grabbed my hand, and with all my family connected and putting all of our powers and energy together, we were able to do the best thing possible.

We jumped up high, and when we crashed down on the ground together, we created a force that would disintegrate anyone in its path, which is why my dad created a forcefield around everyone else. The force was stronger than an earthquake, and could break the bones of anyone in its path. It could shatter eardrums and make people go blind. When the force rippled out, fire came with it. And all of this happened to the monster. And this force defeated it.

CHAPTER 3: STOP THE HATE

"We're now seeing a new America! This past summer, the Splendid Saba defeated a monster at the White House. They tell us that the monsters they've been defeating represent different types of hatred in America. By defeating these monsters, we have now seen a greater America! We see an America with no hate crimes, no gun violence, no gangs, no police brutality, no more school shootings, no more racial hatred, and no more bullying. Different individuals have come forward and said that they are finding that redlining no longer exists. The income and education gap has decreased, and more people are getting the adequate medical care that they need. The Splendid Saba were given a real Presidential

Medal of Freedom ceremony. The President of the United States had this to say…"

A newscaster was saying this on the news today. My mama sent me the link so I could watch it from my phone. Life had somewhat gone back to normal. Mama and Pops went back to work. Ali and I went back to our high school. The twins were now in eighth grade, looking forward to graduating. Lena was almost ready to do some middle school work with the twins. They hated thinking that their little sister would share some classes with them. I had a baseball game, and my team won. Cal won his track meet, Wil won a prize for his graffiti artwork that he created of the Splendid Saba, and Ali won a prize for her writing on why the world needs to be more empathetic. We were all back home in Hyde Park, and America had been a much happier place since we'd defeated the monster. We visited Ahava's grave today, it had been a year since he was killed. I had some things I needed to tell my best friend.

"I've changed so much, Hav. I wish you were here. I realize your death is what drove my family to save America, but it hurts to know that I'll never get my best friend back. I wish you were here to experience a much greater America with me. An America where there is no respect for persons, only respect for all mankind. An America where all men and women are looked at as equal, even though we're all not created equal if you know what I mean. My family is created a bit differently, as you know. We live in an America that is empathetic, that is stronger, that protects, that heals everyone's pain, and that solves everyone's problems. Thank you for understanding me and being my friend. I wouldn't have become the superhero I am today without you." I left my Medal of Freedom at Hav's grave. I felt that we wouldn't have done all of this without him. I had my hoodie, and this time my pops wasn't worried.

When we got home, we saw that my dad had ordered some Giordano's.

"Whoa, Pops you ordered Girdano's? What's the problem?" I asked as we walked through the door.

"Yeah, Daddy, do we have another job to do?" Ali asked.

"No. Everybody, go wash up and then we'll prepare for dinner," my pops said.

"Oh, before I wash up — Ma, can I get a car this year?" I asked my mama as I walked upstairs.

"Boy, stop playin' with me!" my mama said.

"C'mon, Ma, I'm almost seventeen." Upstairs, I got clean before coming back downstairs for dinner. We were all sitting around the dinner table.

"Aight Pops, what's up?" I asked.

"Yeah, I'm confused. Last time we sat down for Giordano's we learned that we would have to fight gun violence," Wil said.

"Well I wanted to start a new trend. I wanted to start bringing Giordano's home as a celebration," Pops said.

"Pops, I really don't feel like celebrating. It's the day Ahava died, and I'm in my feelings right now," I said.

"Right, baby, why are we celebrating?" Mama asked.

"We're celebrating something important. I understand that this is a rough day Bradley, and we're all mourning Ahava's death today, that's why we're all in Black. It's because of his death that we became better superheroes. Losing him made us better, and gave us the ability to fight the monsters we saw before us. We all talked about fighting hatred, and when we think about it, this is what so many before us were trying to do. MLK, Malcolm X, the Black Panther Party, I can go on. And I want to celebrate us being able to bring their goals and dreams to fruition. We worked together to stop something our ancestors worked hard for, died for, and trained us for. We couldn't have done it without God blessing us with these powers and without Jesus dying for us. We couldn't have done it with Saffore's elixir, help, and gadgets..."

"Thank you, my brotha," Saffore said as he came into the dining room.

"What are you doing here?" my pops asked.

"You gave me a key, and I wanted to come and see my family. So I popped up. Y'all bought meat lovers?" Unc asked.

"Yeah Saff, it's in the kitchen," my pops said as he shook his head.

"I'll be right back," Saff walked out of the dining room into the kitchen.

"Anyway, we wouldn't have been able to do this with Ahava. Alright family, dig in," my pops said.

"Thanks, Daddy!" Lena said.

"Hey Ma, I know you wanted all of us to write, or draw, or write lyrics about how we felt. But what did Lena do?" I asked.

"Oh, she made a video today talking about how she felt. Lena's handwriting is not the best. Even though baby girl has a high IQ, she still writes like a seven year old. So I told her she could make a video," Mama said.

"We all should've made a video," Ali said.

"Maybe next time," Mama said.

"Mommy, can we watch my video after dinner?" Lena asked.

"Sure, baby!" Mama said.

After dinner, we all sat down in the living room to watch Lena's video. Mama told us it was short.

CHAPTER 4: CHILDLIKE INNOCENCE AND EIDETIC MEMORY

"Hi everyone, I'm Lena, and I love unicorns, rainbows, the color pink, pizza, and ice cream. But what I love the most is my family. We're all superheroes. Being superheroes is the best. We even got to stop hatred in America. All of my brothers and my sister believe different things about hatred. But my sister Ali was the one who was right. She told me hatred is a monster, and it was. A big monster that is usually people — well, what looks like people, and combines to make a monster. Excuse me, I need a juice box, I'll be back in a sec… Okay, I'm back, oooh it was half a second this time. Anyway, being a kid in America now is great.

Everyone seems to care about each other, play together, no one bullies each other, and everyone seems to be happy. I don't have to worry about being shot anymore, or any of my friends being shot anymore. And we were able to defeat the monster because of my powers. I got all of my powers earlier than my brothers and my sister. Because of my speed, I can create a lot different things. When my family's power and energy combine, it makes all my powers come out. It's like they make me stronger. So the power that light can do comes out in all of us. It makes it stronger. I love being a superhero. So cool!" Lena said. It's like she was shouting during the whole video.

"Your video is great niecy wiecy!" Uncle Saff said, eating ice cream.

"Yeah I love it!" Ali said.

"Us too," The twins said.

"Good job, little sister," I said.

“Thank you everyone! So Mama, who are we going to help next?” Lena asked.

“I don’t know, baby! Maybe we’ll go to a different part of the world and fight their monsters,” my mama said.

“You think we’re ready for that, Mama?” Wil asked.

“I think you guys can do anything,” my mama said.

“That sounds like a good idea! I would love to see a different part of the world and fight against their problems as well,” Ali said.

“Yeah, and I still want my own superhero name,” Cal said.

Ring. Ring. Ring.

“Is that the superhero line?” I asked.

“I think so, I had forgotten all about that ring,” my pops said.

“Answer it, baby!” my mama said. “Maybe it’s the chief telling us that other countries want us to come fight their hatred monsters.”

“Are we ready for that today, Viv?” my pops asked.

“If it’s what we’re supposed to do,” my mama said.

“Hello?” my pops said. “Oh hello, Mr. President!” my pops said we all ran over and he put the phone on speaker.

“Hello, Splendid Saba! You gave me your superhero line so whenever I had a problem I needed you all to solve, I could call you,” the president said.

“Yeah, of course, Mr. President. What do you need?” my pops said.

“Because of your great work defeating hatred in America, I wanted to ask you all about a new challenge,” the president said.

“Sure, Mr. President, what’s the challenge? We’re up to it,” my pops responded.

“Human trafficking. What can you do about it?”

About the Author

Prior to becoming an author, writer, publisher, and doctor of early childhood education, Dr. Ariel Sylvester, Ed.D. guided and taught children in many capacities in public and private sectors in Chicago, Illinois where she was born and raised. She was an after school care teacher, summer camp teacher, apprentice teacher, substitute teacher, temporary assigned teacher, and full-time teacher. Her longest teacher role was a 2nd grade teacher with Chicago Public Schools at a school that she previously attended as a child. Ariel is also an activist for single-mother college students and helping them complete their collegiate degrees. She has ambitious goals of helping them to break poverty cycles and create educational attainment cycles for them and their children. She is also the sole proprietor of Pretty Nerd Publishing. If you enjoyed this book, please read some of her other books listed on her publishing company's website prettynerdpublishing.com.

www.ingramcontent.com/pod-product-compliance
Ingram Content Group UK Ltd.
Pitfield, Milton Keynes, MK11 3LW, UK
UKHW021052270726
13967UKWH00012B/589

9 781958 240274